Girls,
GUILTY
But
Somehow
Glorious

Also by Sue Limb

Girl, 15: Flirting for England
Girl, 15: Charming But Insane
Girl, (Nearly) 16: Absolute Torture
Girl, 16: Pants on Fire
Girls, Muddy, Moody Yet Magnificent
(Previously published as *Zoe and Chloe: Out to Lunch*)
Girls to Total Goddesses

Girls, GUILTY But Somehow Glorious

SUE LIMB

BLOOMSBURY

LONDON BERLIN NEW YORK

Bloomsbury Publishing, London, Berlin and New York

First published in Great Britain in 2007 by Bloomsbury Publishing Plc
36 Soho Square, London, W1D 3QY

This edition first published in 2009

Previously published as *Zoe and Chloe: On the Prowl*

A CIP catalogue record of this book is available from the British Library

ISBN 978 1 4088 0194 9

FSC
Mixed Sources
Product group from well-managed
forests and other controlled sources
Cert no. SGS - COC - 2061
www.fsc.org
© 1996 Forest Stewardship Council

Typeset by Dorchester Typesetting Group Limited
Printed in Great Britain by Clays Limited, St Ives plc

1 3 5 7 9 10 8 6 4 2

www.bloomsbury.com/childrens
www.suelimbbooks.co.uk

For Bessie Carter

1

FRIDAY 1.45 P.M.

Seven days to the earthquake . . .

'We could always . . . just not go,' I said. We were crossing the schoolyard at change of lessons.

'Not *go*???' cried Chloe. 'Not *GO*? Zoe!'

'I only thought . . .' I said, offering her a piece of my chewing gum, 'we could maybe just kind of ignore it. I mean, stay in and watch the football, or something.'

Zoe scowled. 'But what about all those poor homeless earthquake victims?' she demanded. 'The Earthquake Ball's not just for fun, it's to raise money, yeah? Besides, I hate football! *Hate it!*'

Hmm. It had been a mistake to mention football. I quite like a spot of footie, myself. I enjoy watching England losing gallantly. I might even paint the

St George's flag on my face, one day. It would hide the spots – especially the massive zit which keeps resurfacing again and again on my chin (I call it Nigel).

But Chloe's not into football. In fact, she's not really much into any kind of sport. If you throw her a ball, somehow it tends to hit her on the nose, and if you force her into a pool, she swims like a mad little dog in a panic.

'OK, not football, sorry,' I said. 'But maybe a DVD?'

'Oh nooooo!' wailed Chloe. 'We *can't* miss the Earthquake Ball! The Ball is gonna be where it's at! Think of the music! The noise! The headaches! The vomiting! The jealousy! The fights! The broken hearts!' Her face had a wistful, faraway look. In her imagination, she was already *there*.

'OK, then,' I said. 'Yeah, let's go – I was just being stupid.' I shrugged amiably. One of us has to be chilled out, and clearly, Chloe could never play that vital role.

'Yes,' said Chloe. 'We're going. That's obvious. *Obvious!* But here's the major prob: who's going to take us?'

I tossed another piece of gum into my mouth. It's

amazing how quickly it loses its charm. I offered a piece to Chloe.

'No!' said Chloe. 'My brace, remember?'

'Sorry, sorry,' I said. Chloe's brace had been such an epic ordeal. 'Does it hurt at the moment?' I asked.

'No, but I've got to have it adjusted in a couple of weeks' time. I'd rather do maths for the *rest of my life* than have my brace adjusted *for even two minutes*.'

She looked anxious. Maths is one of her very worst ordeals. Or, as she might put it: 'Maths is two of my very worst ordeals.'

Chloe sighed, and snuggled more deeply into her fleece. Though fresh, the air was also almost freezing. We plunged through the swing doors into the warmth of the corridor.

'Who in the world is going to take us to the Ball, though?' said Chloe miserably. 'If we can't find a couple of boys to go with, we'll be social rejects.'

'What about Fergus and Toby?' I pondered. 'They'd probably take us. If we paid them.'

'Fergus and Toby?' screeched Chloe in horror. 'Nothing personal, I mean they're great guys . . .' she looked round furtively, to make sure neither Fergus nor Toby had inconveniently appeared. 'I would rather walk down the high street wearing *only* an old man's trilby hat than go with either Fergus or Toby.'

'What's wrong with them?' I asked. I quite like Fergus and Toby. They're in our class and they're a laugh.

'Zoe, they're so immature, they're practically foetuses!' whispered Chloe. 'I mean, Fergus is a microbe!'

'I think you may be exaggerating just a tad,' I said, laughing. 'He perched on my hand to peck up a few crumbs yesterday and he was definitely heavier than the average microbe.'

'Fergus is approximately five centimetres high,' insisted Chloe. 'And Toby is technically a cream bun. I mean, we're talking serious lard here.'

'Harsh,' I objected. 'Toby's cuddly. Not that I want to cuddle him – no, no! I'd rather cuddle your dog.'

'Zoe,' said Chloe, putting on her mock head-mistress voice, 'dogs are not allowed at the Earthquake Ball. You cannot go to the Ball with Geraint as your escort. People would talk.'

I laughed, but the problem remained. Why did everything have to be so difficult?

Then – oh God! – the swing doors at the far end of the corridor opened, and somebody walked towards us. Oliver Wyatt! Oliver tall-dark-and-haunted-looking

Wyatt! Ashcroft School's answer to Heathcliff. I instantly forgot all about the Earthquake Ball.

My Heights Wuthered. My heart turned into a caged jaguar. A firework display went off in my chest. Whole flocks of butterflies flew out of my ears.

'We *can't* go with anybody from our year,' Chloe said. She looked thoughtful. She hadn't noticed Oliver. *Hadn't noticed.* She was ransacking her bag.

'Hmmm,' I said. The god was strolling towards us. He was a mere metre away. I didn't look at him, of course. I looked at the floor. I knew every detail of his appearance by heart anyway. He didn't stop. He didn't speak to us. He was totally unaware of my spotty, sad, nerdy little life.

I noticed a tiny patch of mud on the side of his right shoe. What wouldn't I give to be that tiny patch of mud! The air stirred up by him swirled around me. There was a faint smell of limes. (His aftershave, obviously: he isn't a greengrocer.) I inhaled deeply, hoping to capture that divine scent for ever.

'We have to corner somebody in the sixth form,' said Chloe. 'They've got to be sixteen or over. I'm too young for a toyboy. Ah, there's my phone. I thought I'd lost it again.' She turned to me and frowned. 'What's up?'

'Oliver Wyatt just walked past!' I whispered. Chloe's eyes flared excitedly. She turned round. She was just in time to see his back disappearing through some swing doors.

'God! Sorry I missed the sacred moment!' She grinned. 'Did he throw you a contemptuous look of burning passion?'

'Certainly,' I informed her. 'But I'm not quite sure whether it's me he loves, or Nigel.' I fingered my chin anxiously. I could feel Nigel lurking there. He'd gone to ground for the past couple of days, but I could sense he was planning to erupt again, possibly on the left-hand side. If one must have a Nobel-prize-winning zit, it at least should be central. For absolute zit perfection, symmetry is essential.

'Have you seen Jack yet today?' I asked. Chloe has a major crush on Jack Bennett, this wicked guy who can break-dance on his head – and let's face it, what else could one possibly ask of a potential husband?

'I don't know . . .' pondered Chloe. 'I haven't felt quite the same about him since I saw him peeing in that alley after the Cramp gig.' Chloe's so easily put off. She can fall madly for somebody at lunchtime and find them loathsome by nightfall. I wouldn't be put off if I saw Oliver peeing. I know he'd pee in a divine, stylish way which would turn it almost into an art form.

'OK,' I said, reluctantly abandoning thoughts of Oliver, 'let's get started.' We had to find a couple of fit partners for the Ball.

'Right, then,' sighed Chloe. 'Where *do* we start?' She offered me a piece of chocolate. I accepted. I think it's good for the brain.

'We start by drawing up a shortlist.'

The bell rang. My heart sank. It was time for German. I don't object to Germany or the Germans at all in principle, it's just that for the first few lessons, when we were starting out, I didn't pay attention. I am a bit of a dreamer, I admit it.

And when, after a couple of months, I sort of woke up and started to concentrate, it was too late. The rest of the class were deep in the book *Das geheimnisvolle Dorf* and stuff like that and I knew that the moment had passed and I would never, never, be able to speak a word of German apart from one rather special one. I could more easily communicate with Chloe's dog, Geraint – by barking.

'OK,' said Chloe, 'let's make the list in German.'

I groaned. 'God, no!' I begged. 'Please, not in German! I just can't cope with it.'

'I didn't mean we were going to make the list in German, Zoe,' giggled Chloe. 'I meant we're going to make the list in *German*!'

2

FRIDAY 2.30 P.M.

Making a list of love gods . . .

Frau Leibowitz the German teacher is a sporty-looking old bird. Well, when I say old, I mean, like, possibly twenty-nine. But despite her muscles and bouncy walk, she is strangely timid when it comes to dealing with us snarling beasts. Plus she has a ludicrously squeaky voice.

'Today,' she peeped, 've are goingk to do translation. Bessie, pliss giv out ze papers. Here you haf a passage I haf printed from ze Internet. *Eine Fahrt mit der Eisenbahn.*' There were a few sniggers. Some people just haven't got over it yet: the German for a journey is *Fahrt*. I haven't got over it myself. In fact, I was one of the people sniggering.

'I am going to make a *Fahrt* to Paris,' I whispered.

Fergus was sitting in front of me and he turned round. Fergus looks rather like a pixie. He has slightly pointy ears, a mop of curly hair, and a cute turned-up nose.

'ThatWouldBeAnOlympicRecord!' he whispered. 'WouldItStillCountIfItWasWindAssisted?' Fergus talks so fast, there's no time for gaps between the words. He was giggling so hard, his curls were actually shaking. Frau Leibowitz ignored us.

'You may use your dictionaries,' she squeaked. Then she sat down and started to mark a huge pile of papers.

We found the passage. The first sentence was: '*Eine Fahrt mit der Eisenbahn kann ich beim besten Willen nicht als Reise bezeichnen.*' I feel really sorry for the Germans. Their language sounds like a house being demolished. I'm glad I'm not doing French, though. Two of the other classes in our year group do French. You have to make really disgusting sounds in French. As if you're wrestling with phlegm.

Chloe and I were sharing the book, which enabled us to conduct a simultaneous written conversation on some rough paper. Although Frau Leibowitz is weedy and timid, nobody actually messes about much in her lessons, because if she gets any trouble she sends

16

people to Irritable Powell straight away. That's Mr Powell, Head of Year. His shouting can cause actual cracks in concrete.

'How about Henry Lovatt?' I wrote.

'No!' Chloe scribbled in reply. 'Terrible teeth. Impossible to snog without serious injury.' Chloe herself has slightly goofy teeth, so I guess this is a factor in her choice of boys. It would be terrible to be separated for ever by matching overbites, your tongues waggling helplessly in mid-air.

'Robin Elliott?'

'Sweat smells like Camembert cheese.'

Chloe started to translate the German passage, so I thought I'd better have a go, too.

'I'd like to ask Gus MacDonald,' Chloe wrote five minutes later, 'but he is rumoured to have a tartan penis.'

That did it. A laugh burst out of me: a truly disgusting snort. Frau Leibowitz looked up crossly.

'Zoe!' she said. 'Pliss stop being schtupid!'

'Sorry!' I said, wiping my nose with a very ragged tissue from my pocket. 'It was a sort of sneeze gone wrong.'

Frau L ignored this and went back to her marking. I began to browse through the German dictionary. I looked up buttocks. It was *Hintern*. I looked up green. It was *grün*. I looked up polka dots. They weren't in the dictionary. It was a shame, because I was planning a slightly amusing sentence about Chloe's bum.

We walked home with Fergus and Toby. They were arguing about football. Chloe pulled her football face. She's really pretty with masses of freckles, dramatic green eyes, and a wild bunch of red hair. But when she pulls her football face (eyes crossed, tongue lolling out sideways) she manages to look like some primitive life form which has just crawled out of a swamp.

'If you say one more word about sport,' she warned the boys, 'we won't ever share our crisps with you again.'

Predictably, they laughed in an infantile way as if she'd said something obscene. Chloe was right about boys our age being toddlers. The boys went on ahead, still arguing about a missed penalty.

'I think you were a bit harsh about Henry Lovatt,' I said to Chloe. 'OK, his teeth are sort of very much out there, but he is kind.'

'Kind?' said Chloe, looking puzzled. 'What do you mean?'

'We were in the cafeteria once,' I said, 'and I couldn't find a place. And he gave up his seat for me. OK, he had sort of finished, so he was going to get up anyway, but he got up kind of quickly and smiled at me.'

'Oh my God!' said Chloe, grinning. 'You must be married at once, before people start to talk.'

'What's the goss then, girlz?' asked Toby, waiting for us up ahead and pouting cutely. He puts on a camp voice most of the time, and he does a hilarious impression of Sharon Osbourne. Toby's plump and smiley. His hair is flicked up in a series of cute little wisps and his eyes are huge and blue. He has lovely rosy cheeks covered with blond down, like a peach, and his lips are big and rubbery.

'Mind your own business,' said Chloe sniffily.

'It'sBrilliantIt'sBrilliant!' said Fergus. His voice goes even more squeaky when he's excited. Chloe once said Fergus is like a cartoon character, which suits him perfectly.

'What is brilliant?' Chloe asked.

'We'veGotThisBrilliantIdea!' said Fergus. 'We're GonnaBringABlow-upDollIntoSchool, DressItInSchool Uniform, FillItWithHeliumAndLetItOffInAssembly. It'llLike*Fly*RoundTheHall!'

'God, I can hardly wait,' I said drily. 'And where are you going to get the helium?'

'eBay!' yapped Fergus.

'You are sick idiots,' I said, but with genuine affection. 'Why don't you get a life? Learn to play chess, or bandage the legs of old women in Africa, or something?'

'In my gap year,' said Toby, 'I'm going to bandage legs like there's no tomorrow. Only they're going to be rich legs. Old ladies in Vegas. I'll give them a massage and a manicure, and they'll be fighting over me. I'm gonna be married by the time I'm twenty – to a gorgeous ninety-year-old millionairess.'

At this point we turned a street corner, not far from the infamous Dolphin Cafe where, when we can afford it, we hang out after school. A couple of sixth-form guys were strolling towards us: Donut Higgs and Beast Hawkins.

Donut's real name is Phil, but everyone calls him Donut because he's such a lard. His head is shaved and his face is like a potato, complete with scabs and hairy warty bits. His breath smells of sick. Apart from that, he's a real babe-magnet.

As for Beast, he's a big muscular rugby player with long greasy black hair, strange magnetic grey-green eyes, and a reputation for complete depravity.

As they strolled past us, Beast winked at Chloe. They don't ever talk to us but sometimes Beast gives us a horrid grin or something. Once they'd gone past, Fergus and Toby started to make howling noises. This is traditional with Beast. Everywhere he goes, people howl like dogs.

'Let's hear it for Beast Hawkins,' said Toby. 'He's an animal!' And he threw back his head and yowled.

'OneOfYouTwoShouldMarryHim,' gabbled Fergus. 'ThenYourKidsWouldBeHalfHumanAndYouCould SellYourStoryToThePapers.'

'You idiot!' said Chloe with a nervous giggle. 'I wouldn't ever even soil the sole of my shoe by *walking over* Beast Hawkins. He's half in prison already.' But then something slightly strange happened. She blushed.

I noticed, because I'm very interested in colours. I know everybody's interested in colours, sort of, but I'm obsessed by them in a deranged kind of way. Chloe's complexion is normally porcelain-pale, apart from the freckles. Most redheads are like that.

But for a few seconds after the mention of Beast Hawkins, Chloe's face went an interesting shade of pink. Not shrimp pink, not shocking pink, not shell pink – oops, sorry, I mustn't let myself get carried away. Anyway, she blushed. I decided to mention Beast Hawkins later, sort of casually, and see if she blushed again.

Fergus and Toby didn't notice, of course. They had found an empty drinks can lying on the pavement and had reverted to football. They were competing, as they walked along, to see who could kick an empty can furthest along the pavement. There was quite a lot of jostling, which Toby mostly won, as he is large. But Fergus was small and nippy and darted in and gained possession of the can several times.

'Why do boys do that?' I asked.

'It's biology,' said Chloe. 'My mum says males are programmed to storm about doing violent things to the environment.' Chloe's mum is a bit of an old hippie, and she loves the environment a lot more than she loves Chloe's dad. He's hardly ever at home. He works in Dubai, which suits Chloe's mum just fine.

'Men!' I sighed. 'Our only hope is to round them all up and sterilise them.'

'Yes!' agreed Chloe. 'We'd have to save a bit of sperm, obviously, to continue the race.'

'Ben Jones's?' I suggested, with a massive Jonesian sigh.

'Ben Jones's, obviously,' said Chloe with another, even bigger sigh.

'I know he's only in our year,' I said, 'but we could ask him to escort us to the Earthquake Ball.'

'Dream on, Zoe,' said Chloe sadly. 'There's a waiting list right around the block just to be spat on by Ben Jones. And you know he never goes to anything with anybody. Except that stupid Mackenzie.'

'Perhaps they're *lovairs*,' I said in a seductive French accent.

'Well, if they are, all I can say is, lucky old Mackenzie!' said Chloe.

At this point we reached my house. It's completely ordinary. The front garden has a couple of bushes and some gravel. My mum sometimes refers to this as 'the shrubbery' and she gets very cross when people throw crisp packets over the wall.

'Hey, guys!' I called to Fergus and Toby, who were still wrestling and kicking over possession of the dented can. 'Wanna come in for a coffee?'

'NoThanks!' said Fergus. 'Dan'sGotANewGame!'

'Yeah,' said Toby, 'we're going to destroy the universe for a couple of hours over at his house.'

They went off, still kicking the can. Chloe watched them for a moment, thoughtfully.

'We so *can't* go to the Ball with Toby and Ferg,' she sighed. 'Which is a shame, because they're really sweet guys. But they're like, totally and utterly *not* Ball material.' She was right.

I opened the front door and immediately smelt coffee. That meant Dad was home. I just hoped he wasn't wearing *those* trousers.

3

FRIDAY 4.30 P.M.

Dad gives v. bad advice . . .

'Hi, parent, I'm home!' I yelled, waltzing into the kitchen. There was a faint distant growl from upstairs. Dad was evidently up in his study writing. He designs computer programs, although his actual full-time occupation is drinking cups of coffee.

Luckily Chloe and I could talk undisturbed because my mum hadn't come home yet. She travels around being a hotshot executive. It's something to do with insurance. I wish my parents had more romantic jobs. If only Mum was Editor of *Vogue* and Dad was some kind of celebrity TV chef. Or an actor. That would be so cool. People would come up to me in school and say, 'I saw your dad being abducted by aliens on TV last night. He's got such charisma!'

There was a note on the table in Dad's hand-writing:

MRS NORMAN RANG: CAN YOU BABYSIT ON SUNDAY?

My heart sank. The Norman twins are terrifying. OK, they're only pre-school, but already homicide is their main interest. I dread being alone with them, and as often as possible I take Chloe along as back-up. However, their parents pay well and I was saving up nicely for our summer trip to Newquay. Already I had £137.

'Babysit with me on Sunday,' I pleaded. 'It's those little monsters down the road.'

'Hmmmn, possibly, OK,' said Chloe. We are both terrified of the Norman twins, but if I had Chloe by my side at least they wouldn't outnumber me.

'OK,' I said, getting a couple of cans out of the fridge, 'first, let's make a list of the boys who are way, way out of our league, just fantasy figures.'

'What's the point of that?' sighed Chloe. 'We'd just be torturing ourselves.'

'All the same,' I insisted, 'Let's just put them down, at the top of the list. Under, er, *"Boys to Die For"*. Oliver Wyatt and Jack Bennett?'

'I've gone off Jack Bennett,' said Chloe. 'I told you

about the peeing. I never, ever want to see my husband in the loo. It would be unbearably foul.'

'Well, put Oliver Wyatt down,' I insisted. 'I haven't gone off him, and I'm sure he pees with style and grace.' Briefly I went into a kind of dream in which Oliver swept me up on his white horse and galloped off towards a glamorous castle where I just knew he was going to kiss me for hours by a log fire, with owls hooting outside. 'I wish I was aloof and mysterious, like Oliver,' I sighed.

Chloe smiled to herself, and wrote: *Oliver Wyatt: not available, as he is too grand for girlfriends.* 'I don't understand what you see in him, Zoe,' she said.

'Charisma?' I suggested.

'Hmmm.' Chloe frowned. 'Charisma? I don't think so. He's just tall and quiet, really. You might as well date a lamp-post.'

A little flicker of annoyance went through me. OK, I love Chloe to bits, but she knew she shouldn't ever diss Oliver.

'How about Beast Hawkins?' I suggested, with a sudden bitchy flash of inspiration. Well, she deserved it.

'Beast!' exclaimed Chloe. 'Ugh! Horrid! He should be on a list of Boys Who Are Half-Human.'

And then she blushed! Again!

'You fancy him!' I yelled. 'You do! I saw you blush!'

'I do not!' Chloe screamed. 'Ugh! Ugh! He's unbearably gross!'

I grabbed the pencil and drew a heart with an arrow through it. On one side I put 'Chloe' and on the other, 'Beast'.

'Stop it! Stop it!' Chloe was laughing hysterically, and trying to rip the pencil out of my hand. It went flying across the room. Then she grabbed the paper, screwed it up, and tried to force it into my mouth. 'Eat your words, Morris!' she cackled hysterically.

At this point my dad came downstairs. I'd been hoping he wouldn't be wearing the burgundy shirt and the jeans that are too young and too tight, but of course he was. He appears when he's hungry, although all the time he's working up in his study, he's snacking for England on cheese and biscuits and cups of coffee. I jumped up and gave him a hug.

'Love you, Dad!' I said. 'But I've told you before: those jeans are a mistake!' I spend hours with my big sister, Tam, leafing through fashion mags and trying to work out which Armani suit would make Dad look like a million dollars.

'Listen, Zoe, I'm a style disaster,' said Dad. 'Get over it. Hi, Chloe!'

Chloe greeted my dad rather politely. She's a bit shy of him, probably because her own dad's away so much on business, she doesn't have much practice at Dad Talk.

'Guess what, girls,' said Dad, 'I just did a quiz on the Internet. Apparently, I'm officially obese. So I'm going on a diet, starting tomorrow.'

He ripped open the fridge door and looked inside, drooling. My dad is one of those parents who think they have to entertain children. This is fine, and even delightful, until the child is about ten. Then, the cringing starts.

'What sort of day did you have at school?' he asked, feasting his eyes on a cold chicken.

'Fine, OK,' I said, assuming he was addressing us rather than the dead hen. 'How about you?' I have to say this, otherwise apparently it's not polite.

'Terrible writer's block all day,' said Dad. 'I've been watching daytime TV, snacking every five minutes and doing quizzes on the Internet.'

'What's your latest project?' asked Chloe politely.

I prayed. *Please, God, don't let Dad get started on his work.*

'It's about Computational Physics and Physical Chemistry,' he said.

Chloe and I groaned in stereo.

'Don't say any more about it, Dad,' I begged. 'Like, *ever*.'

'Sorry you've had a crap day, though.' Chloe frowned. She was only being polite, of course. When I go to her house I'm polite in the same way when her mum, Fran, launches into a passionate account of her struggles with the zodiac.

'It's awful, Zoe,' she said to me last week, 'I can't get the right colour curtains, because I'm an air sign and Chloe's a fire sign, so we're totally incompatible. I want pale gold curtains, but Chloe needs to be surrounded by red.'

'Tragic!' I sympathised. I didn't dare tell her that red and gold were both totally wrong, in fact her whole curtain project was doomed, and she should dump the lot at a jumble sale and invest in pale, latte-coloured linen. (Tam and I spend hours reading Mum's interior design mags, too.)

'Yes, my work sucks,' said Dad thoughtfully, ogling a chocolate mousse. 'I'm thinking of getting a job in a shoe shop. You staying to supper, Chloe?'

'Er – not if it's chicken, sorry,' said Chloe. She's a

very picky eater.

'How about nachos?'

'Sorry,' cringed Chloe. 'I don't like Mexican food.'

'How about fishcakes?'

Chloe looked deeply disturbed. 'Er . . . I can't eat fish, sorry,' she said. 'I'm allergic to it.'

'Oh really?' said Dad, tearing his eyes away from the fridge for a moment and staring in fascination at Chloe. 'What happens if you eat fish, then?'

'Don't ask, Dad!' I yelled. 'It's disgusting! Just let Chloe have some beans on toast or bread and jam and cereal. That's all she ever eats, remember?'

'Oh, yeah,' said Dad, turning back to his beloved food. 'Fine, OK.'

'I *do* like chocolate, Zoe,' said Chloe almost indignantly, as if I'd done her a major injustice.

'The rest of us are going to have spaghetti,' said Dad, getting out a chopping board. 'Zoe, lay the table. Mum'll be back in half an hour.'

'Where is she?'

'She's on the train.'

'Well, I can't lay the table yet,' I objected. 'We haven't finished our list.'

'What list is this?' asked Dad.

'It's hopeless,' said Chloe. 'We've only got a week

31

to find a couple of boys to take us to the Earthquake Ball. Most of the boys we know are horrible and nerdy, and the few who aren't are way out of our league and already bagged.'

'Oh, never mind,' said Dad light-heartedly. 'You could put up a postcard on the supermarket notice-board. Or hire a couple from an escort agency. Or go to a football match and recruit a couple of hooligans. OK, that's sorted. Now get off the table! I'm going to chop onions.' He switched on the radio and searched for onions all over the kitchen, while listening to the news.

'My God! Your dad's so right!' hissed Chloe. 'He's so brilliant – honestly, you are lucky. My parents are rubbish by comparison.'

'He was being ironical,' I told her.

'No, no!' whispered Chloe. 'Your dad's right. We should think laterally. OK, all the boys we know are nerds or out of our league. But what about all the boys we *don't* know?'

'Oh. I see . . . yeah,' I mused. 'There must be a couple of boys somewhere in this city who are, like, tolerable.'

'And it's our job to find and fascinate them,' said Chloe. 'Before they've had time to realise how nerdy *we* are.'

'It's a challenge, all right,' I said. 'But I fear we have no choice.'

'It's either that,' said Chloe, 'or go to the Ball alone and needy.'

'I'd rather swim a mile through sick than go to the Ball alone,' I shuddered.

'OK, then,' Chloe whispered. 'After supper we go up to your room and draft an ad.'

4

FRIDAY 8.45 P.M.

We set a cunning trap

After supper we went up to my room. My teddy bear Bruce was lying with his legs in the air and a big smile on his face. Chloe grabbed him and cuddled him.

'I so adore Bruce!' she sighed. 'If only we could find a magic-potion thing that would turn him into a boy.'

'You'd have to fight me for him,' I warned her. 'And anyway, Bruce is gay.'

Chloe laughed, kicking off her shoes and diving on to my bed with Bruce. 'OK then, let's draft the ad!'

I still had some misgivings about actually advertising for boys, but I got a piece of paper out and sat down at my desk.

'It seems a bit tacky,' I said. 'How do we word it? *"Romeos wanted"*? *"Must be gorgeous and fragrant with perfect manners"*?'

Chloe bit her nails and frowned. 'I know!' she said. 'We don't actually tell them we're auditioning them to be escorts to the Ball. We advertise for something else. Uhh . . . *"Boys wanted for odd jobs"*.'

'It sounds weird,' I said, biting my pen. There was a lot of biting going on. I had a feeling that before we managed to draft the ad, we'd be eating the furniture.

'It sounds weird advertising for *boys*, plural,' said Chloe. 'We'll probably get more than one reply anyway.'

I wrote: *Boy wanted for odd jobs*. It still looked a bit strange. 'Hmm, it doesn't say anything about age,' I said thoughtfully. 'It would be awful if we were deluged with a lot of little Boy Scouts.'

'*"Odd jobs"* sounds a bit weird, too,' pondered Chloe. 'It doesn't sound, like, inviting.'

'Yeah . . . maybe we should try and make it sound mysterious and intriguing.'

'Hmm.' Chloe lay on her back and stared at the ceiling. Chloe's great when it comes to throwing ideas about. She can think on her feet. And she can also think on her back. 'How about, *"Young man wanted for exciting venture"*?' she suggested.

I wrote it down. It was certainly better than *Boys wanted for odd jobs*. In fact, if I was a young man I'd certainly be interested.

'*"Venture"* is good, too,' I mused. 'Because it doesn't necessary imply big bucks.'

'We're not actually going to pay them, are we?' asked Chloe, sitting up suddenly. 'I mean, we can't! I thought the idea was, get to know them by pretending we've got a job offer, and then once we've fascinated them, they'll be begging to take us to the Ball.'

'Or we could keep it as a strictly business arrangement,' I said. 'I mean, we might not be able to fascinate them. We might not *want* to fascinate them. They might be perfectly OK, but just not heart-throbs. How much do you think we should pay them?'

'I don't think we should pay them,' said Chloe. 'I think we should sweep them off their feet!' OK, so she's great at brainstorming, but she can be a bit silly at times.

'We *could* pay them, though, in theory,' I went on, 'if it was *necessary*. We could dip into our Newquay money.'

'Hmmm,' Chloe looked a bit doubtful. 'I don't

want to waste my precious holiday money on a guy to take me to the Ball. Not if I can get him to take me for nothing.'

'OK,' I said. 'You fascinate yours, and I'll pay mine.'

The final draft of the ad, after about a hundred more versions, went like this:

Strong, fit young man (over 15) wanted for exciting weekend venture.

Then we had an argument about whose mobile number we were going to give.

'You're always losing your mobe!' I said accusingly.

'I'm not!' objected Chloe.

'OK, then. Where is it right now?' I'd seen her put it down on the kitchen dresser before supper and I knew she wouldn't remember.

'Oh God!' Chloe went pale. She searched her pockets. Then she ransacked her bag. She even started looking under my bed, which was pretty stupid. 'Oh my God, Zoe, it's gone!' she cried, approaching a major panic.

'I think you'll find it downstairs on the kitchen dresser,' I said in an irritating know-it-all kind of way.

Chloe ran downstairs and came back up with it.

'You pig, Zoe!' she yelled, laughing, and pushed

me over on to the bed. 'You knew where it was all the time and you just sat back and watched while I had a total panic attack!' She started to tickle me. I screeched wildly. I am incredibly ticklish. Sometimes my sister, Tam, can make me scream for mercy just by stalking up to me with her tickling fingers poised and a sadistic gleam in her eye.

'Stop, stop!' I gasped. 'I'm sorry! Stop! Anything! I'll do anything, just as long as you stop!' Chloe stopped. I sat up, panting and wheezing.

'You're right, though,' said Chloe, carefully putting her phone in the specially designed phone pocket inside her bag. 'I think we should put your mobile number.'

We both knew her phone wasn't going to stay in that pocket for long. All too soon it would be off on its adventures: the top of the loo cistern, the fruit bowl, the pyjama case . . .

'And another thing.' I was really thinking fast now. I was cooking on gas. 'Maybe we should give false names just in case . . .'

'In case what?' asked Chloe.

'Well, you know, it's all a bit iffy.' I was trying to create exit strategies. 'If somebody rings up and sounds like a complete moron, or it's someone we know, and we know they're a moron . . . we can just tell them the position's taken and if we use false names, they'll never even know it was us.'

'Brilliant!' yelled Chloe, clapping her hands. 'I've always wanted a different name. I'm going to be Africa Zanzibar.'

'Don't be an idiot,' I sighed. 'That's so obviously an alias.'

'OK, then,' said Chloe. 'Africa Stevens.'

'Does it *have* to be Africa?'

'Well, there are two girls in school called India,' argued Chloe. 'And I met a girl called China on holiday. And, you know, Paris and stuff. What's wrong with Africa anyway? I think it's a cool name.'

'OK, OK.' I knew I had to give in. But to show Chloe how to operate with tact and skill, I decided to call myself something really subtle, like a Jane Austen heroine.

'I'm going to be Emma Collins,' I said.

'That's so lame!' objected Chloe. 'Anyway, there's a girl in the sixth form called Emma Collins.'

'I'm just trying to be subtle,' I explained. 'Unmemorable. Not interesting. So if we want to dump them before we've even interviewed them, they won't care. I'll be Jane Elliott, then. I mean, nobody would care if they weren't going to meet a Jane Elliott. But if they'd psyched themselves up to meet somebody called Zebra Zanzibar, well – they'd be crushed.'

'Zebra?' cried Chloe. 'Zoe, you're brilliant! Zebra's even better than Africa! Z. Z.! What cool initials! Or maybe I could have three Zs? Zebra Zara Zanzibar? That would be mega!'

Chloe easily gets over-excited. She's just completely at the mercy of her emotions. I think they call it 'mercurial'. I was going to have to raise my voice to her. Just a tad.

'For God's sake, Chloe!' I almost-snapped. 'You're going to be Africa Stevens and I'm going to be . . . uhhhh, Jane Elliott.' My name was so dull and ordinary I'd forgotten it already. I added our aliases to the draft of the ad. Chloe accepted the Africa identity and we moved on to the next argument.

We disagreed about how the ad should be designed: Chloe wanted it festooned with stars and moons and God knows what. I just wanted it to be plain print, because I thought that was a lot more mysterious. I talked her round in the end.

Chloe stayed the night, as it was Friday. She sleeps on a blow-up mattress on my floor. 'A bit like a pet dog,' as she always says. Chloe's dog Geraint actually sleeps on the bottom of her bed. I'm so jealous. I've got no hope whatever of having a dog. Not until I'm twenty-one, anyway. And I have to *earn* it . . . but that's another story.

We decided to put the ad up on the noticeboard in the supermarket the next day.

'The ad might not work,' I said, after we'd switched out the light. 'But it doesn't matter. I mean, we shouldn't just *rely* on the ad. Nobody at all might answer it.'

'Oh, absolutely!' said Chloe. 'I mean, I think we should try everything. All sorts of different ways. Stop guys in the street, the lot. We've got the whole weekend. Toilethead are playing at Plunkett tomorrow night.'

'Right!' I was beginning to believe we could really sort this out. 'Let's swoop down and snatch our unsuspecting victims there.'

5

SATURDAY 10.44 A.M.

Hunting for boys – the new blood sport . . .

On Saturday morning we put our postcard up on the supermarket noticeboard. Then we trawled round the charity shops, hoping for some divine designer cast-offs. There weren't any. We had jacket potatoes with cheese and beans for lunch. Then we went back to Chloe's and watched some DVDs. Finally, after a quick tea of beans on toast, it was time to get ready for the Toilethead concert. Obviously, this took hours.

I wore a fab black dress which minimises my tum, and some huge hoop earrings. I blitzed my hair into submission with heavy-duty wax (I've inherited Dad's spirally curls, which is a total pain.) I applied a lorry-load of eye make-up in order to smoulder sexily at boys we didn't yet know. And I plastered an inch-thick layer of heavy-duty cover-up foundation over Nigel, who, with perfect timing, had re-emerged on my chin that afternoon. Nigel was throbbing, almost *flashing*. Life is so unfair.

Chloe has all the physical advantages. Slim hips, slender legs, a tiny waist, skin as white as milk, etc. Luckily she has atrocious dress sense and on this occasion was wearing khaki cropped combat trousers and a hideous lime-green T-shirt saying 'A Present from Weymouth' on it. Her strange little triangular boobs were certainly not enhanced by this outfit: in fact, they were virtually invisible.

She was wearing wedges, and I have a horrible suspicion they were her mum's wedges left over from the last century. To complete the style disaster, she had scrunched her hair back into a horrid plait-thing stapled to her head. I wouldn't dream of telling her, but she looked like a Victorian child pickpocket called Dick Dickens.

We were, however, determined to pull. We hit the Community Centre at 8.45 p.m. precisely. Toilethead were already in full swing – even as far away as the bus station, the pavements were vibrating. Once inside, we went straight to the girls' loos, where a thousand sweaty females were feverishly applying lip-stick. We applied some too. Standing next to us were a couple of girls from our year group: Flora Barclay (aka the Goddess Venus) and Jess Jordan (Comedy Legend).

We said hi and I thought how tough it must be for Jess, having a friend as drop-dead gorgeous as Flora.

'The trouble is,' Flora was saying, 'I'm not sure if he knows that I know, because last time I saw him he looked at me as if he doesn't know I know, but it all might be just a big act.'

Jess caught my eye in the mirror and winked. It seemed that Flora had communication issues. Well! Who would have thought it?

'The solution,' said Jess, 'is a head transplant.'

'Oh God, yes!' sighed Flora. 'I'd do anything to get rid of these spots!'

Spots? The Goddess had spots? Jess and I exchanged another look – the sort of look Cleopatra's handmaidens must have shared when Cleo moaned about being the frumpy type.

'Oh, you'd still have spots,' said Jess. 'I just meant that if you and he swapped heads, then you'd know what he was thinking.'

'No, I wouldn't,' said Flora ploddingly, 'because

I'd still have my head and he'd still have his.' She is good at maths, apparently.

Jess rolled her eyes to heaven, and prepared to leave the mirror. She gave me a goodbye grin.

'Enjoy!' she said. 'It's a zoo out there.'

They left, and I started to check out the lipstick situation. Chloe's was the wrong shade of pink – a horrible coral colour – and she'd got some of it on her teeth. Although she does have most of the physical advantages, this doesn't include her teeth. It's the overbite.

'Oh God!' she said. 'I've got lipstick all over my brace!'

For some reason I didn't need a brace. I have inherited my dad's big white teeth. But when I laugh too much I do look a bit like sunrise over a whitewashed town in southern Italy. I try to cultivate a girlish simper and keep my goddam teeth inside my mouth.

Chloe scrubbed away at her teeth with a tissue, but the tissue got kind of torn and snagged and bits of it appeared to be caught on her brace like sheep's wool on barbed wire.

'Ugh!' she gasped. 'I'm in serious trouble here! My mouth is full of paper! We have to go home again! Now!'

'Don't be stupid,' I said, enjoying a rare moment of superiority. 'Just keep your mouth shut for once in your life. Swill some spit around. The paper will get soggy and come away, and then you just swallow it.'

'Yuck!' said Chloe. 'Gross beyond words! My mouth will become a kind of *toilet*!'

Eventually we went out into the huge dark cavern that is the Sir George Plunkett Memorial Concert Bowl. The band were rampaging up and down the stage. Lights were flashing. Lasers were crawling up the walls. We pushed our way into the crowd.

'I bet Oliver will be here,' screamed Chloe into my ear. 'You can fascinate him!'

'Oliver won't be here!' I roared back. 'He'll be at home grooming his string of racehorses!' I may be fantasising slightly about Oliver's background. He may live in a smelly little house in an alley behind the Dog and Duck, for all I know.

We pushed forward – about halfway to the front where we got kind of trapped in a big clump of giants. Maybe they were a rugby club or something. Bloated faces leered at us as we fought our way past, and hideous guys shouted a series of unappetising invitations. We ignored them in a dignified way. I was beginning to wish I hadn't put on so much sexy smouldering eyeshadow. I scowled, so they'd know I wasn't some kind of trashy airhead; just a lofty intellectual wearing ironic post-modern make-up.

'There's room up front,' said Chloe, turning round and yelling at me over her shoulder. Then her face changed to shock and horror. She gestured wildly, staggered sideways and fell horribly to her right. The inevitable moment had come. She'd fallen off her espadrilles.

I wasn't expecting her to be badly hurt, but Chloe is a little bit of a drama queen. She grabbed her ankle, writhed on the ground and literally howled in agony. People around started to look. I tried to bend down and offer her some help, but my dress was so goddam tight, I couldn't quite make it.

The guy in front turned round. Oh no! It was Beast Hawkins!

'Whassup?' he said, giving me a quizzical look.

'Twisted her ankle or something,' I said.

Beast crouched down beside Chloe. Oh no! Perhaps he was going to mug, rape, murder or pillage her right now! He was mad, bad and dangerous to know – and my helpless friend was at his mercy.

'She'll be all right,' I said. 'It happens sometimes.

47

She's got these very thin ankles and sometimes they give way.'

Beast wasn't listening. My voice was totally inaudible anyway, as Toilethead were in full spate. He had taken Chloe's espadrille off! He looked up and handed it to me. Now he was feeling her ankle, the cad! Chloe was sitting up now, still wincing and swearing, but also staring in amazement at Beast.

I wasn't sure whether he was performing first aid or beginning a seduction. I felt totally helpless. So I just stood and watched. Beast stood up and reached down for Chloe's hands. He hauled her to her feet. Then he put his arm round her waist, and she threw her arm round his shoulders, and he helped her hop back through the crowds.

I followed, carrying the espadrille. And, slightly to my dismay, Beast's companion followed me. It was, of course, Donut, Beast's lardy sidekick. He hadn't said a word to me yet, and I intended to keep it that way.

'Tough,' he said, sort of over my shoulder. 'Still, the band is crap.' I pretended I hadn't heard. I could see what their game was. They were exploiting Chloe's tragic injury in order to pull us. Well, they weren't going to get away with it.

When we got out to the lobby, we could see that

Chloe's face had gone green. This was worrying. And it clashed abominably with her T-shirt. Beast sat her on a low wall by the popcorn booth, and placed the sole of her injured foot on his thigh.

Ugh! He was performing some kind of loathsome sex act with her foot and his leg! I could tell by his face that he was enjoying it. The really annoying thing was that Chloe was ignoring me. And as usual when injured, she was panicking.

'My ankle!' she groaned. 'Look at it! It might be broken! It's swelling up! *Look!* Call an ambulance!'

We looked. Her ankle, previously trim and cute enough to fascinate a whole army of Victorian gentlemen, now resembled a sausage and was steadily expanding.

'Call the *ambulance!*' sobbed Chloe, still clinging, rather recklessly I thought, to Beast's hand.

'No need for an ambulance, babe,' he said soothingly. 'We'll take you to casualty in Donut's car. Bring it round, Doh.'

6

SATURDAY 9.45 P.M.

I break my solemn promise . . .

Donut slouched off to 'bring the car round'. It made
him sound like a manservant – but then, that's the
sort of relationship he has with Beast, or so the gossip
runs. Chloe was sitting on the wall sort of snivelling
and shuddering. Beast was stroking her leg and whispering things to her. I felt decidedly spare. It's usually
my job to look after Chloe and reassure her, but that
job appeared to be taken.

Chloe specialises in injuries and ailments. This was
the third time in our relationship that she had
demanded to be taken to hospital. But I was beginning to suspect she had double motives this time. She
wasn't staring into Beast's eyes or anything gross, but
she was kind of looking down in fascination at his

hands, and listening.

She knew it was her duty to struggle bravely to her feet, grab my arm, and say firmly, 'Come on, Zoe! We'll get a taxi home. It's all right, Mr Beast, or whatever your name is – thanks for your help,' exactly as laid out in the *Anxious Parents' Charter.*

I felt a bit uneasy as the last time I'd been driven by a schoolboy, the car had mounted the pavement and destroyed the frontage of Flowers to Go. We had been unhurt, luckily, but the chrysanthemums were utterly mashed. I had assured my parents I would never go in a boy's car again.

'If you faithfully keep this promise, Zoe,' Mum had said, with her Serious Face on, 'we'll buy you a puppy when you're twenty-one.'

Typical of my family. You have to walk everywhere for six years, until your feet are covered with massive blisters the size of the moon, before you can get your hands on a puppy. Chloe's parents got her a puppy while she was still at primary school. Although Chloe's puppy has turned into the huge and rather sordid dog called Geraint. Much as I envy the puppy idea, I've always been a bit wary of Geraint. Sometimes he behaves as if he's some kind of sleazy boy in dog's clothing.

'It's OK,' I said, asserting myself at last. 'There's no need for you guys to leave the concert. We'll get a taxi. My family's got an account with a taxi firm.'

'Don't worry – Donut's a very careful driver,' said Beast, looking up at me and winking. I wished he wouldn't do that. It made me feel part of a conspiracy or something.

'Zoe!' hissed Chloe unexpectedly. 'Donut has gone for his car now! It doesn't matter! It's only to casualty.' I was amazed at her foolhardiness. She must know that Beast and Donut were planning to drive out of town at 100 mph, over several round-abouts and through several electronics stores without stopping, and eventually mug us and abandon us in a wild wood, stranded without our mobile phones or handbags, in the rain.

'Anyway,' said Beast, grinning, 'the band is crap.'

'Yeah,' agreed Chloe. 'They suck. Ow! My stinkin' ankle!'

Beast caressed her foot some more.

I was astonished. Chloe *adored* Toilethead. They were her favourite band. She had pictures of them stuck on her bedroom wall. She had once collected their autographs on her thigh and hadn't washed for a week. And now apparently they were crap, just because Beast Hawkins said so. Mad, Bad, Dangerous Beast. I was amazed and, needless to say, horrified.

Shortly afterwards, Donut strolled in, carrying his car keys in a raffish, joyriding, hooligan kind of way.

'I'm illegally parked,' he said as if it was the coolest thing in the world. 'So move, guys!' I wondered if it was too late to send a goodbye text to my parents. A deep sense of doom settled over me.

Somehow Beast got into the back of the car with Chloe, and I was sure he was going to be holding on to and stroking several other bits of Chloe as well as her ankle. This meant I had to sit in the front with Donut. I glanced sideways at him. His warts were worse than ever. He grinned at me, and his teeth flashed greenly in the streetlights.

'Listen,' I said. 'Please don't drive fast, because I get carsick.'

'Don't worry, babe,' he said. 'I used to be a speed freak but since I wrote off the last car I'm a reformed character.'

He started the car. I shrank back in my seat and prepared to meet my Maker. But what was this? Donut edged the beat-up old banger ever so gently out into the city traffic, and drove like a sweet old lady down towards the hospital.

'So,' he said, 'what you doin' later?' I was torn between the desire to keep him in a good mood because he was driving, and the desire to tell him to take a running jump.

'I have to go home,' I said, 'and babysit for my two little brothers. Because my parents are going to a nightclub later.' It was easy, inventing both younger brothers (I was thinking of the dreaded Norman twins) and a parental lifestyle. A nightclub! My parents' idea of fun after 10 p.m. is a cup of cocoa and a DVD of *Miss Marple*.

'I'm a five-star babysitter,' grinned Donut, looking as if he habitually ate five babies for breakfast.

'Sorry,' I said. 'No Followers. It's a strict rule of the house.' I was a bit pissed off that Chloe wasn't backing me up. It was so quiet in the back, I wondered if she and Beast were actually snogging or something. I was so tempted to turn round and have a look.

'Followers?' said Donut. 'Whatdjer mean?' Though a sixth former, he was clearly intellectually challenged.

'It's just one of my parents' stupid jokes,' I explained. 'Back in the Victorian era, there was, like, a No Followers rule for servants. Like, they weren't allowed to – uh, entertain men friends.'

'Bummer!' said Donut, and sighed unpleasantly.

Suddenly we arrived at the hospital. We drove right up to casualty and helped Chloe out. Then we went inside and registered. Chloe was hanging on to Beast all the time, even though I was there and quite willing to support her. She clearly fancied him like hell. I was disgusted with her – or would be, once I was sure she'd escaped serious injury.

7

SATURDAY 10.28 P.M.

Heart stopping-moment in casualty

We sat in a corner of casualty. Chloe sat between me and Beast. He had his arm round her shoulders. I thought this was a bit of a liberty. So I threw my arm round her shoulders, too. That meant, however, that what I'd done was throw my arm round his arm. He peeped at me behind her back and winked. My God! What a two-timer! He was already flirting with her best friend, literally behind her back!

I had other, more pressing problems: Donut was sitting next to me and his huge thigh was pressing sideways against mine. It wasn't all that different from being snuggled by a fat dog wearing denim. I wriggled grumpily.

'Shove up a bit, can't you?' I said.

'Sorry, babe,' said Donut. 'Crowded in here, innit?'

It was. People were pouring in all the time. Guys with bleeding heads, women with dodgy collarbones, an old lady with a black eye. They all looked worse than Chloe. I wondered how long it would be before she gave up, admitted she was the least hurt of anybody there, and limped off home.

Suddenly there was the sound of a laughing baby. People looked round. Oh no! It was my phone! I have a laughing baby ringtone. I regret it sometimes. I dived into my bag and grabbed it. A number I didn't recognise showed on the display.

'Hello?' I said. On all sides, people were watching.

'Hi,' said a deep sexy male voice. 'Could I speak to Jane Elliott, please?'

'Sorry,' I said. 'Wrong number.' Thank God. I didn't fancy taking a phone call here.

'Uh, wait,' said the voice. 'Is that Africa?' For a split second my memory banks tried to warn me that I ought to know what the guy was talking about. But I was so aware of all the strangers watching and listening that I couldn't concentrate.

'No?' I shook my head sarcastically as if I was being called by a retard. 'It's *England?* I think you must have a wrong number.'

'Sorry. I was hoping to speak to Africa Stevens or Jane Elliott about an advert – some kind of weekend project. My name's Matthew Kesterton.'

'Oh! I'm sorry! Of course!' My heart almost leapt out of my mouth and impaled itself on one of the coathooks by the door. My alias was so damn subtle, I'd completely forgotten it! For an instant there I hadn't even remembered that Chloe was Africa! I was so distracted by all this Beast and hospital stuff, our ad had gone completely out of my head. I felt myself blushing furiously, and struggled to my feet.

'Just a second, sorry . . .' I said. 'I do remember something about this. I'm not Jane, but I could take a message for her, or even maybe . . .' I weaved my way towards the exit.

My mind was racing. What could I say and not sound a total imbecile? Matthew certainly had a charismatic voice, and I didn't want to alienate him totally before we'd even had a chance to inspect him.

'Sorry about that,' I said, as I reached the relative privacy of the corridor. 'I'm Jane's aunt, and I'm in a hospital casualty department. There's been a bit of an accident, and I seem to have picked up Jane's phone by mistake. Wait – she's round here somewhere –

there she is! Jane!' I called out to myself, hoping no one was watching. The corridor was semi-deserted, thank God.

'There's a call for you, Jane,' I said to myself. 'I seem to have picked up your phone . . .' Then I did a bit of dramatic rustling, swapped the phone to my other hand, dug deep and produced a different voice.

'Hi!' I said. 'This is Jane!' I should never have gone squeaky. I sounded like a demented glove puppet on a children's TV show from the 1960s.

'Sorry to ring at an inconvenient time,' said Matthew. 'I hope nobody's seriously hurt?'

'Oh no!' I squeaked. 'It's OK! It's my Aunt Lizzie's friend Bertie.' Where in the world did that name come from? 'He fell off a ladder. He was painting her ceiling. He thinks he might have broken his ankle.'

'Oh God,' said Matthew. 'I'm really sorry.' He was so sympathetic and polite, bless him! Lavishing all his concern on a Bertie who never existed! 'Can he move his foot at all?' asked Matthew. I was getting a bit irritated now. Did Matthew have to pry quite so much into the personal medical records of some-body? Even if that somebody was fictitious?

'Yes, he can move it,' I said, so squeakily my throat literally hurt. 'To be honest, I think it's just sprained.

We can talk about the project, no problem.' No problem apart from ruptured vocal cords, anyway.

'So this project,' said Matthew. 'What is it, exactly?'

At this point I realised that Chloe and I had given no thought whatever to the fictitious 'project' we were going to be pretending to interview the guys about. For an instant I was tempted to shriek an insane noise down the phone or run into the nearest loo and hurl it down the toilet. But Matthew's sexy voice kept me focused – just.

'It's to do with, well, uhhhh,' (I was thinking on my feet, now) 'did you see that programme called *The Life Laundry*?'

'No,' said Matthew. 'Does it matter?'

'No, no,' I insisted. 'It was about, you know, helping people to reorganise their lives, y'know? That's what this project's all about.'

'What's the rate of pay?' Matthew asked – rather cheekily, I thought. Though I suppose if I was applying for a job it would be uppermost in my mind.

'Uhhh, £5.60 per hour,' I said. There was a silence. Matthew was evidently disappointed. I didn't want him to be put off. 'That's the starting wage, obviously, but you know, it could go up.'

'Oh,' said Matthew. He was sounding slightly less than thrilled. I had to keep him interested.

'Look, can you come for an interview?' I asked.

'When?' enquired Matthew.

'Well, how about – tomorrow afternoon?' I was flying by the seat of my pants here.

'What time?' asked Matthew.

'Well, could you make, say 2 p.m.?'

'Sure,' said Matthew. I loved the way he said *sure*. The guy was just dripping testosterone, you could tell. I gave him Chloe's address, because I knew that tomorrow afternoon my parents were going to be hanging about and doing things at home.

I didn't want my dad Trying to Be Amusing or my mum hovering nearby with a Terribly Concerned look on her face while we were trying to conduct a serious interview. Also we hadn't told them about the ad, and I just knew my mum would disapprove. Quite apart from the fact that I would have to be a squeaky Jane for interview purposes, and Chloe was going to have to become Africa.

It would be much easier to do it at Chloe's. Her dad's always in Dubai, and we could easily get rid of her mum for a few hours by telling her a strange star had appeared in the east, or something.

'OK,' said Matthew with thrilling briskness. 'I'll be there.'

Seconds after I rang off, Donut appeared. He seemed even more repulsive after my conversation with Matthew.

'Your mate's thirsty,' said Donut, approaching the drinks machine. I inspected the merchandise.

'I'll get her a sports drink,' suggested Donut. 'Give 'er a bit of a hit, like. High energy.'

'No,' I said. 'Chloe only drinks water or juice.'

Donut laughed in a jeering kind of way. I selected still mineral water and put the money in the machine.

'What's yer name again?' enquired Donut with graceful etiquette.

'Zoe,' I said. 'Zoe . . .' Wait! I *so* didn't want to reveal my true identity, but my recent experience of aliases had left me somewhat bruised and tired.

All the same, it was essential Donut didn't know my real name. I had to think of a fictional surname, but my brain kind of jammed and I could only think of Hitler. Even someone as stupid as Donut might smell a rat if I said I was called Zoe Hitler. 'Zoe . . . Berlin.' It was the names-as-geography thing again. I'd finally succumbed to it.

'Cool, so, uh – whatyer doin' tomorrow night,

Zoe?' asked Donut, looming over me like some enchanted wardrobe.

'Babysitting,' I said firmly.

'For your little bruvvers again?'

'No – the people down the road.' This was true. I had to babysit tomorrow for the terrifying Norman twins. My heart sank at the thought. Being stuck in casualty, chatted up by a hideous hulk was bad enough, but it was as nothing compared to the torment routinely dished out by the dreaded Normans.

'Where d'you live?' asked Donut. It was absolutely vital I didn't reveal my real address. I just knew he'd be round there, parking his heap of metal and slouching menacingly up the path to our helpless, innocent house.

What sort of address should I invent? Should I go for somewhere posh, so he'd feel intimidated and back off in case my dad, Lord Berlin, horsewhipped him? But if I was posh, he might be even more turned on. He might think, *Hmmmm. Pull this little darlin' and you're laughing, mate. Skiing holidays, Porsche, the lot.*

On the other hand, if I invented a life of picturesque poverty he might think that because I was trailer trash, he could do what he liked with me and nobody would care. Or even worse, he might make it his mission to rescue me from the mean streets and come round with charitable bags of hamburgers and his mum's cast-off clothing.

'I live . . .' I hesitated. I was hopelessly poised between the devil and the deep blue sea. 'I live in . . . Blue Street.'

'Blue Street?' frowned Donut. 'Where the 'ell's that?'

'It's in Devilsham,' I said. 'A bit out of town. Over towards Deeping. In fact, we live on a farm. Way out in the sticks.'

'A country girl, eh?' said Donut, horribly charmed by my ludicrous lies. 'Got any haystacks where you live?' I would have backed off, but the wall was behind me. 'Tell you what,' said Donut tenderly, 'you're a well fit bird. Fantastic earrings.' And he lifted a podgy finger and touched my sacred hoop earrings! Earrings given me last Christmas by my sacred sister, Tamsin, reading social sciences at Waveney Wessex College!

I edged sideways to get away from the podgy finger, and then to my utter astonishment, a face appeared behind him. A pale face. A handsome face.

A haunted face. It was *Oliver Wyatt*! Strolling down the corridor towards us and carrying, bizarrely, a bunch of lilies. Our eyes locked. My heart reared up like a demented humpbacked whale, butted me ferociously in the tonsils, then plunged back with a thunderous lunge towards the deep blue sea, which lay somewhere in the region of my pelvic bones.

Oliver Wyatt looked at me with perfect indifference, because, of course, he had absolutely no idea who I was. He did, however, recognise Donut's back, and tapped on the thuggish shoulder with magnificent, imperious disdain.

'Donut!' he said. Donut turned round – still, catastrophically, holding on to my earring. Oh no! Oliver was going to assume I was some kind of trashy hanger-on of Donut! I had to make it clear that for him to fondle my earrings was completely out of order.

'I hate them!' I said treacherously (and quite painfully), tearing off my earrings. 'They're *so* not me! You can have them if you like! Give them to your girlfriend!' OK, it was obvious. But I was desperate. So desperate, my words had come out in a horrible chavvy shriek.

Oliver looked down at me with mild astonishment,

as if I had picked my nose or possibly hawked and spat on the hospital floor.

'Nah, leave it!' said Donut cheerily, refusing the earrings. He noticed I was staring at Oliver with foolish longing. If only Oliver would swoop down and rescue me right now! Was his white horse tied up in the hospital car park? It was time for him to act, dammit!

'This is . . .' Donut struggled to remember my name. 'Jade Burley.'

'Jade Burley?' I snapped. 'I'm Zoe Morris, you idiot!' I shot Donut a contemptuous glance and turned to Oliver. 'What's your name, in case he gets it wrong?' I enquired, in what I hoped was an arch, witty and sophisticated manner.

'Sir George Plunkett,' said Oliver. Donut laughed a horrid snorting laugh.

'He isn't!' chortled Donut. 'He's Olly Wyatt, innit? Who's the flowers for, Olly? Some fit bird havin' your baby or summink?'

Oliver looked offended and slightly embarrassed. 'My mother's just had an operation,' he said. 'What are you doing here?'

'Her mate's bust her ankle,' said Donut, indicating the nearby casualty ward with an oafish toss of the head. Oliver frowned slightly and looked sympathetic.

'Hope it's OK,' he said to me. For an instant he looked right down into my face. His eyes were deepest brown. It was as if a chocolate fountain was raining down on me.

'Oh, she'll be OK,' I said. 'Chloe's just got weak ankles. I hope your mum gets better soon.'

'She'll be fine,' said Oliver. 'So – Donut. Are you coming to the Next Big Thing tomorrow?' The Next Big Thing is an annual party, just for the sixth form.

'I dunno,' said Donut. He looked down at me. 'Are you comin', darlin'? Or are you gonna be tied up milking the pigs?'

'I can't come,' I said, with what I hoped was waspish distaste. 'I'm not in the sixth form.'

'Wait . . .' Oliver's eyes had turned in my direction. 'Pigs . . . ?'

'Jade lives on a farm,' said Donut, putting on a stupid yokel voice. ''Er's a milkmaid or summat.'

'Really?' said Oliver, staring at me with something approaching fascination. 'You live on a farm, Jade?'

'Zoe,' I said. Although why I wanted him to get my name right, in the midst of so many lies, I really can't say. 'Well . . . yeah.'

'What livestock have you got?' asked Oliver.

A random menagerie of weird animals stampeded through my brain. Antelopes, giraffes, the snow leopard.

'Oh, the usual,' I said. 'You know. Pigs, cows, sheep and stuff.'

'Really?' Oliver looked more and more interested. 'A mixed farm? Is it organic, by any chance?'

'Oh, yes, of course.' I had a feeling this would turn Oliver on even more. 'Organic as it gets. Dung everywhere.'

'Listen,' said Oliver. 'I'm going to do vet science at college. I'm looking for a farm to work on in the holidays.' My heart performed a kind of sizzling somersault of horror and delight. Oliver wanted to work on my farm! Except I didn't have one!

He reached inside his jacket and fished out a card. He handed it to me. Our fingers briefly touched. I would never wash my hand again.

'That's my number,' he said.

I scrabbled in my bag and gave him my numbers too. My fingers brushed against his again. A thrill ran from my fingertips right down my back. This was weird, magic stuff.

'Ask your dad if he needs extra help in the

holidays, and give me a ring?' he suggested.

I nodded dumbly.

Oliver looked eagerly down at me. His eyes were shining. But I knew it was only at the thought of my fabulous pigs. 'Well,' said Oliver, with perfect aristocratic grace, 'got to go. Bye, Jade.'

'Zoe,' I said. 'Bye.'

'See you, mate,' said Donut.

And Oliver was gone. I wasn't sure whether it was the worst evening of my life so far, or the best. I'd spoken to Oliver! Actually had a conversation with him! And there was a way to spend the whole of the holidays with him! All I had to do was acquire a farm. I'd certainly have to put in a lot of babysitting over the next few weeks.

'C'mon, then,' grunted Donut. 'Your mate'll be dyin' of thirst.'

Good God! Chloe's drink! I'd almost forgotten Chloe existed. In my imagination I was romping in the hay with Oliver.

I couldn't wait to tell Chloe I'd actually spoken to him. But I knew I'd have to wait until after her X-ray. And after we'd managed to get rid of Beast and Donut. If we ever *did* manage to get rid of them.

8

SATURDAY 11.08 P.M.

Late-night heartache in the rain . . .

As I entered the waiting room, Chloe was hopping towards me. She had that intense look on her face which I have come to dread.

'Gimme the water!' she hissed. 'I'm parched!' I handed the bottle over. She unscrewed and swigged.

'It was a rip-off,' I said. '80p. Robbery.'

'OK, OK, I'll pay you tomorrow,' said Chloe. She was suddenly talking differently since she'd met Beast. She sounded somewhere between a cowboy and a gangster. It didn't suit her. She's supposed to be nervous and refined like the heroine of a Victorian novel. 'Listen,' she said, grabbing my arm. 'My ankle's not broken. I can, like, tell.' In other words, it had stopped hurting. 'And all these people need a doctor so much more than me!' she whispered, casting a quick glance round the assembled wounded. 'So the guys are giving us a lift home.'

'The guys?' I asked, cocking a sceptical eyebrow. Beast was hovering so close, I couldn't let rip with my real feelings, which basically would have gone like this: *Are you mad? Totally mad? You know that Beast is famously the most depraved animal in the entire sixth form – and you've agreed to let his sub-human sidekick drive us home??? So they'll, like, know exactly where we live???!!!*

I had to find a formula which would let me off the hook, without going into quite so much detail about Beast's reputation. He was leering at me, only centimetres away, clinging to Chloe's arm.

'Don't worry, babe,' he said. 'You'll be safe as houses. Donut was taught to drive by the Queen's chauffeur's cousin's brother-in-law!'

Chloe laughed: a mad, whirling sort of laugh, as if she was drunk.

'Sorry,' I said. 'I have to go back to the concert. I'd arranged to meet somebody there.'

'Who? You never told me!' Chloe's eyes flared.

'We can pick him up,' said Beast, with a naughty grin. 'If your heart's set on him, why not? The more the merrier! We could drop in at Pasquale on the way home! Who is the geezer?'

'Nobody you know,' I said airily. 'He's at St Kenneth's.'

'What! A posh git?' Beast laughed a wheezy, horribly attractive laugh. 'I say, Donut old boy, bring the Rolls round. And don't forget the bacon!' Donut and Chloe laughed with passionate abandon. I didn't find the situation remotely funny.

'Who is it?' asked Chloe. 'Who's this mysterious toff you've got lined up, then?' She also laughed a wheezy laugh, as if she was copying Beast's.

'I'll tell you, if you promise not to reveal his identity,' I said. I placed my lips to Chloe's ear and shielded my mouth with my hand.

'If you want to go mad and put yourself at the mercy of these Neanderthals, fine. But count me out. Oh, and the boyfriend's Prince Michael of Spamelot.'

Chloe lurched away from me and started to look cross and tearful. Beast watched her like a hawk, and then turned his eyes on me.

'OK, then,' she said, with just the hint of a tremble. 'You go back to the concert, and I'll go home.'

'We have to talk about that phone call just now,' I

said. 'We got an answer to our ad. I said we could do the interview at your place tomorrow at two. OK?'

'Fine, fine,' said Chloe, flapping her hand as if what I was saying was an irritating fly. I could tell she wasn't really listening. There was a slightly stressy atmosphere.

I managed to wriggle out of the lift back to the concert. Chloe was bundled into Donut's old heap and they tootled off. I saw her face at the window: pale, pissed-off and accusing. From her point of view, I'd abandoned her.

From my point of view, she'd abandoned me. I hobbled down the road towards the Toilethead concert. My shoes were starting to pinch me. I took them off and walked barefoot. It started to rain.

As I reached the venue, I realised I didn't want to go back there anyway. There was no Prince Michael of Spamelot, there was no Chloe; what was the point of piling back into that smelly crowd? I hesitated, and decided to get a taxi home. I just had to call home first, to make sure it was OK to pay on arrival. I knew Mum and Dad wouldn't mind.

Just as I was getting my mobile out, it rang. My sister, Tamsin! Major delight! She'd be able to put all my troubles in perspective and give me tons of mature and insightful tips on how to handle Chloe's sudden madness. And I *had* to tell her that Oliver had spoken to me! She'd be thrilled to *smithereens*!

'Tam, you legend!' I yelled. 'How's uni? What's going on?' She usually had some bizarre but stylish pranks to report.

'Uhhh, hi!' she said. She sounded a bit down. 'Yeah, well . . . you know. Problems, problems.'

'What problems?' I asked. 'Presumably it's *lurve*?' Hastily I racked my brains for the name of her latest beloved. Tamsin tends to flit from one flirtation to the next. Then I remembered. It was some research guy called Tom. She'd been quite smitten. In fact, she hadn't rung me for a couple of weeks.

'No,' said Tamsin. She sounded evasive. Kind of mysterious. 'It's nothing to do with relationships. Well, not directly. Look, Zoe, can you come up for a couple of days?'

'How about tomorrow?' I asked. 'Oh, no, wait, I'm babysitting.'

'Tomorrow's no good anyway,' said Tamsin. 'I've got an essay crisis. If I'm late with this one Gina will take out a contract on me.'

It's odd how, when you're at uni, you address your teachers by their Christian names but they're still kind of frightening and stuff.

'Next weekend, then?' I asked. Tamsin did not reply. In the background I could hear the melancholy wail of a police siren. It made it all so much more depressing and film noir.

'It's ages till next weekend,' said Tamsin edgily. 'I need to see you, like, right away.'

'Look, I'll come next Sunday, right? Next Saturday's the Earthquake Ball. I'll come up the day after. Just look after yourself till then and give yourself lots of treats,' I told her maternally. 'Make yourself a cup of hot choc. Watch your Bridget Jones DVD. You know that always cheers you up.'

'I'm sick of Bridget Jones,' sighed Tamsin. *Sick* of Bridget Jones? Tamsin must be seriously depressed. 'I've just got to find a way out,' she went on, in a funny kind of flat voice, as if she was almost talking to herself. 'I'm just going to walk and walk all night in the rain . . .'

'Don't be stupid!' I said. 'You'll catch your death of cold and get mugged, raped and murdered.'

'No, no, I'll be fine,' said Tamsin in a faraway voice.

'Now listen, Tam,' I said urgently. I was earning a gold star for motherliness. 'If you do that, I won't be able to sleep all night. I'll tell Mum and Dad, and they'll go mad with worry.'

'Don't you DARE mention anything about this to Mum and Dad!' snapped Tamsin, suddenly wide awake and right in my ear. 'Promise me you won't say anything at all! Don't even mention my name!'

'OK, OK,' I said, rattled. Why wouldn't she tell me what was bothering her? It sounded really serious: she didn't want Mum and Dad to know. I was starting to feel sick with worry.

'Where are you now?' I asked. 'Right now?'

'Uhhh . . .' There was a strange blast of sound. I think it was Tamsin blowing her nose. 'Down by the river.'

My blood ran cold. The river! *Please, God, don't let her throw herself in*, I prayed.

'Listen to me, Tam!' I yelled. 'Go back to college and go round and see Parvati. She'll look after you.'

'Parv's got glandular fever,' sighed Tamsin. 'She's gone home.'

'Well, somebody else, then,' I went on. 'Emma. Laura. Jemima.'

Tamsin's only reply was another huge sigh, then suddenly the phone went dead. I tried to ring back but got through to her voicemail.

'Call me back,' I said. 'Any hour of the night and day. Go back to college now and have a cheese sandwich. You know it makes sense. Love you!'

Phew! So much for my big sister being wise and composed and putting everything into perspective for me. I leaned thoughtfully against the wall of the leisure centre and put my shoes back on. This evening seemed endless, and my heart was heavy as lead.

'Hey! Zoe!' I looked round and saw two familiar figures: one small and pixie-like, the other looming large with flicked-up fair hair and an earring. Toby and Fergus. They glared grumpily at the night sky.

'Hi, guys!' I said. 'Share a taxi home?'

'Sure,' said Toby. 'Where's Chloe?'

'She pulled,' I said grimly.

'Oooo, nice!' said Toby. 'Anyone we know?'

'Only Beast Hawkins,' I said. Toby and Fergus looked amazed.

'He'llHaveMadeHerIntoAPieByNow!' said Fergus.

'Almost certainly,' I said, hailing a passing cab. 'But that's not our problem. So: what did you think of the concert?' I asked as we piled in.

'ItSucked,' said Fergus. 'ToiletheadHaveGoneDown ThePan. Appropriately.'

'Plus we got *nul points* for seduction,' said Toby. I stared. Were Toby and Fergus on the pull?

'Did you have anyone special lined up?' I enquired.

'Nope,' said Fergus. 'WeWeren'tFussy,BelieveMe. AndWeStillDidn'tScore. AlthoughIDoThinkThatGirl InTheTarpaulinFanciedYou,Tobe.'

'Yeah,' said Toby. 'She was gagging for it. But she was covered with lovebites and smelt like a chicken farm, so regrettably I had to suppress my lust.'

'Hey! Never mind, guys,' I said. 'Tomorrow is another day.' It was kind of weird, imagining little Fergus and camp old Toby actually chatting up girls.

For the rest of the journey I lapsed into a thoughtful kind of trance. I stared out of the taxi windows. The rain was lashing down in the dark. It streamed across the glass like tears down somebody's cheeks. I was anxious about Tamsin. I rang her again, but her phone was switched off.

Once Fergus and Toby had been dropped off and I'd got the taxi to myself, I took out Oliver's card. It didn't give his address: just his mobile number and email address. I instantly memorised them, and tucked the card down inside my bra, next to my heart. I would kiss it later (the card, not my bra or heart) once I was alone in my room. I didn't want the taxi driver to see me actually snogging cardboard.

When I got home, I went straight up to my room, turned on my PC and went online. I did a search on farms for sale. The cheapest I could find was around £450,000. It looked really nice and had two big barns for the pigs that Oliver adored. And the good news was, I would be able to afford it. I just had to babysit for 288 years, first.

9

SUNDAY 2.00 A.M.

A dangerous breakfast looms . . .

I couldn't sleep. I tossed and turned. I counted sheep – our sheep, on our farm, me and Oliver. My brain was absolutely raging. I didn't know whether to obsess about Oliver, worry about Tamsin and Chloe, or wonder how on earth we were going to interview Matthew for the 'life coach' job. Every half hour, I checked my mobile. I even rang Tamsin at 2 a.m., I was so worried about her. Her mobile was still switched off.

Finally I fell asleep. But then, horrid dreams had me in their spell. I was chased through deserted streets. My legs wouldn't move. Men with paper bags over their faces loomed out of alleyways, begging and clutching at me. Then I was at a funeral, but I wasn't sure if it was Chloe's or Tamsin's. Then a live frog jumped out of my pocket. Then a pterodactyl crapped on my head. It would have been less exhausting to stay awake.

Eventually I woke up, dragged a few clothes on and lurched downstairs. My mum, looking elegant in her kimono, was sipping coffee and reading the style section of the Sunday newspaper. Dad was making scrambled eggs and smoked salmon.

'How was the concert last night, darling?' enquired Mum, offering me her smooth and fragrant cheek to kiss.

'Oh, cool,' I replied. Parents must never know if an event is a total nightmare, because they might not let you go next time. 'Can we sell this house and go and live on a farm?' My parents looked startled.

'A *farm*?' said Dad, still stirring the eggs. 'I thought teenagers liked towns.'

'Not all teenagers,' I said. 'Actually I'm thinking of becoming a vet.'

My parents exchanged what I believe is known as a Significant Glance. Mum put the newspaper aside.

'But you hate science,' she said. 'Especially biology. You said so only last week.'

'That's because I'd bombed in that test,' I said.

'Anyway, I've changed my mind. Can we sell this house and go to live on a farm? Can we sort it all out before the summer holidays?'

'Count me out,' said Mum. 'With *my* hay fever? Are you mad?'

'Count me out as well,' said Dad playfully. 'I'm frightened of cows.'

'Seriously, Zoe,' said Mum, pouring more coffee, 'farming is a profession. Well, a calling, almost. You need specialist skills. You need to be the outdoor type. Well, look at us.' She shrugged, and looked at Dad. He was holding a wooden spoon and wearing a pinny decorated with fluffy clouds. 'And anyway, farms cost a fortune. Our little house isn't worth anything. You couldn't even get a single cow into our front garden.'

'Not unless you folded it up and ironed it,' said Dad eagerly. He likes ironing.

'But farms have hundreds of acres,' said Mum. 'Land costs money. We could never afford it, even if we wanted to.'

'And we don't want to,' said Dad. 'So that's that. Next question?'

I made myself a cup of tea.

'Next question,' I said eventually, tucking into a

piece of toast, 'Did Tamsin ring you last night?'

'No,' said Mum. 'Why? Is something wrong?' She went pale.

It's no use trying to keep anything from Mum. She may look like a jet-setting businesswoman on the surface, with her sleek suits and her state-of-the-art laptop, but underneath she's some kind of Stone Age ape-mother, defending her babies from the sabre-tooth tiger. She's also a tiny bit psychic, but unfortunately it doesn't work when it comes to the lottery.

'She rang me on my mobe last night,' I said. 'She's fine. I just wondered if she'd rung you as well.' I smiled brightly.

Mum flew to the phone and dialled Tamsin's mobile. I just went on eating my toast. Dad and I rolled our eyes at each other.

'What are your plans for the rest of the day?' he asked, in a mock polite voice, like somebody on a train you've never met before.

'Homework and babysitting,' I said. 'In other words, fabulous excitement from beginning to end.'

'What homework?' he asked. He's always hoping it will be something he can help me with.

'Oh, nothing,' I said. 'Just Hitler, you know. The rise of Hitler.'

'Hitler *again*!' groaned Dad. 'You seem to do nothing but Hitler! What is wrong with the exam boards?'

Meanwhile Mum got through to Tamsin's voice-mail. 'Hi, darling!' she trilled in a light-hearted voice. 'How is everything? Hope you're OK, and if you're feeling a bit tired, don't forget we'd love to have you home for a day or two and give you lots of TLC.'

'And toast!' said Dad.

'And Dad says toast!' said Mum. 'He sends his love. Ring us when you get a min. Lots and lots and lots of love.' She put down the phone and sighed anxiously. I prayed that Tamsin's mobile wasn't lying at the bottom of the river. 'Zoe!' said Mum sharply. 'Have you tidied your room? I want to take a load of stuff to be recycled. What about those old clothes you were sorting out for the Oxfam shop?'

'Yeah, yeah,' I groaned. 'I'll do it today – after my history homework, OK?'

Whenever Mum's worried about Tam, she has a go at me. It's not fair, being the young one. You're still there, in the firing line, after the glamorous first-borns have all gone swanning off to their cool and stylish lives at uni.

With no hens to milk or pigs to scratch, I had little

choice but to embark on 'Hitler's Rise to Power'. Well, obviously, I did spend half an hour selecting the right colour lipstick, first. One can't study the Third Reich wearing just any old pink. In the end I selected a kind of bruised 1940s secret sinister pink with brown overtones.

I texted Chloe: **DON'T FORGET WE'RE INTER-VIEWING SOMEBODY CALLED MATTHEW AT 2 p.m. YOUR PLACE.**

There was no reply. Maybe Fergus and Toby were right, and Beast had already made her into a pie. Eventually I really got into Hitler. I had a fantasy that I was a secret agent. I pretended I was a glamorous typist. I had my hair done in two sausages each side of my head, and I wore a figure-hugging satin dress in dove grey. I was blonde, obviously. You had to be blonde, in those days. It was Go Blonde or Be Exterminated, almost. Mind you, sometimes I think life in the twenty-first century's a bit like that, too.

I wormed my way into his good books by flattering him with witty badinage, as we strolled on the ramparts of his mountain hideaway. *That moustache!* I would enthuse. *I so love the way it's just as wide as your nose!* I was planning to assassinate him with a stiletto hidden in my cleavage, when my mobile phone rang – or rather, laughed. I grabbed it.

'Hello?' said a faraway voice. 'I'm ringing about the advert.'

Oh God! Another one! At least this time I was in private. Because I'd been through such hell with Matthew over the aliases, I decided that if the issue of names came up, I'd quietly ditch Jane and Africa.

'Oh, right, yes, hello,' I said briskly. 'What's your name?'

'Scott Nicholls.' He sounded nervous, but somehow sensitive and intriguing. He sounded dreamy. He sounded like a poet with long curly hair and passionate grey-blue eyes.

'Right, Scott,' I said, 'We're starting a life coaching company. We'll be turning people's lives around. Giving them, er . . . control. The work will be varied. And fascinating.'

'Oh,' said Scott. 'Right.'

'We're doing some interviews this afternoon, if you could possibly make it?' I enquired. God, I was so efficient. In part of my brain I'd already convinced myself that I *was* starting a life coaching company. Never mind Oliver Wyatt – I was rapidly falling in love with *myself* as a thrusting young executive.

'Yeah, I could make this afternoon,' said Scott,

evidently postponing his plans to wander pensively by some daffodils. I gave him Chloe's address and suggested he come at three. It was all fixed.

Amazing! Our ad had only been up for twenty-four hours and already we'd got *two* candidates, and they both sounded fabulous in their different ways. I wasn't sure which I preferred. Matthew sounded masterful and macho, as if he would look after me. Scott sounded attractive and vulnerable, as if he would require looking after. Either way, I was game. Chloe and I might have to end up tossing a coin.

My phone laughed again. This time it was Chloe herself. I couldn't wait to tell her all about Scott and Matthew.

'God, Zoe!' she whispered. 'Sorry I didn't ring earlier. I lost my phone. I just found it now in Geraint's basket. I didn't want to use the landline because I didn't want Mum to overhear.'

'Overhear what?'

'Well, last night Beast said, well . . . uh, I know it sounds uhhh, a bit over the top, but he said I was *beautiful*.'

'Watch out!' I protested. 'Beast is bad news. You know that. He's famously a heartless cad. Frankly I'm amazed you can still speak this morning, after all the heroin sandwiches he must have forced you to eat on the way home last night.'

'Don't be silly,' giggled Chloe. 'All they did was drive me home, but Beast was whispering these things ... we were in the back, and Zoe, he *snogged* me!'

'What!?' I was disgusted, shocked and panicky. 'What? *Really?*'

'Yes! And he asked for my phone number!'

I was worried. Chloe is easily swept off her feet – especially when wearing espadrilles.

'Listen,' I said. 'Be really careful.'

'Of course, of course,' said Chloe, trying to sound sensible. 'He'll probably never ring me anyway. He probably treats all girls like that.' You could tell by her voice that she was lying, and that she wouldn't be able to eat or sleep until he rang her. 'So what's all this about the interviews?' she asked, sounding almost really interested.

I quickly briefed her on the Scott and Matthew scenario, and she said it would be fine to interview them at her house. Her mum had gone off to spend the day with some friends.

'So, no probs?' said Chloe, rather dreamily.

'Well, there is a problem, actually,' I told her. 'Last

night, at the hospital, I actually got to talk to Oliver Wyatt – out in the corridor by the drinks machine.'

'Really?' said Chloe. 'Wow! Well done you!' But you could tell she was thinking about something else.

'But I've got myself into a really stupid dilemma.' I cringed at the thought that Oliver was waiting for Dad's phone call inviting him to come and work on our farm. I was just about to tell Chloe all about it when she interrupted me, ignoring all mention of my dilemma.

'Beast is really just a pussycat,' said Chloe.

I gave up. My best mate was clearly obsessed and deluded. What really bothered me was that if Beast was the pussycat, poor little Chloe was certainly the mouse. I've always felt a teeny bit responsible for Chloe, and I knew with a sickening certainty that, at any moment, he was going to pounce. And I wasn't going to be able to do a thing about it.

10

SUNDAY 12.33 P.M.

It came from outer space

When I got to Chloe's house she had lunch ready – the inevitable beans on toast. Then we spent an hour making ourselves look fabulous and businesslike by tying our hair back and applying a lot of red lipstick. Chloe tried to get away with cargos and a T-shirt, but I soon forced her into a pencil skirt and a nice crisp blouse. I was wearing a plain black dress, and some chunky silver jewellery.

We tidied up Chloe's sitting room. We polished the coffee table, plumped up the cushions, and arranged pens and paper, so we could make notes.

'I keep thinking we really *are* doing a job interview,' giggled Chloe. 'When do we tell them the job is really just taking us to the Ball?'

'Hmm . . . I don't think we should say anything like that in the interview,' I said. 'No matter how gorgeous they are. I think we should act as if it really is about being a life coach.'

'Yeah . . .' agreed Chloe. 'But – but how do we wriggle out of it later?'

'I'm not sure,' I said, feeling a bit doubtful. 'Let's just play it by ear.'

'What if we don't like them?'

'We just ring them later to tell them the position's been filled,' I said, thinking fast and trying not to panic.

'You'll have to do that,' said Chloe, shuddering. 'No way could I tell people they're dumped!' I sometimes wonder how she'd manage without me to do all the dirty work. But in a funny kind of way, I like being the one who can actually hack it, while Chloe watches admiringly from a place of safety.

Suddenly Chloe's doorbell rang with a horrid nerve-shredding BAZZZZ! It's not very spiritual really. I'm surprised her mum hasn't got a yak's bell from Tibet or something.

'You go!' whispered Chloe, going pink and sort of cringing as if she was hiding in mid-air. On my way through the hall I passed a mirror, and took a quick peep. I looked like someone auditioning unsuccessfully for the Matrix. Unfortunately Nigel had surfaced and was pulsing away on my chin like a road sign. What kind of life coach can't even control her own complexion?

Nigel wasn't the only throbbing little item in my repertoire. Suddenly I remembered the aliases. Oh God! I was going to have to conduct this interview as Squeaky Jane. Maybe it would be sensible to give up right now, before we even started. Maybe we should send Matthew away and apply to become nuns.

My heart was pounding anxiously as I opened the door. Matthew with the thrilling masculine voice was about to appear. I could hardly wait.

A strange, rather plump boy stood there. His fair hair was slicked back, and he was wearing a suit and carrying a briefcase. His face was pasty, and he didn't smile. He held out his hand.

'I'm Matthew Kesterton,' he said. We shook hands. His hand was cold and limp. Ugh! I already knew I could never, *never* go to the Ball with him, because of his horrid cold hands. I was *so* tempted to wipe mine on my dress, to get rid of the cold limp feeling, but somehow I managed to refrain.

'Come in, Matthew!' I squeaked, with heroic

poise. I led him into the sitting room, where Chloe was waiting. She looked jittery and mad. Her eyes were more huge and green than ever.

'This is Africa,' I said, in the voice of a tiny cartoon character. Chloe kind of twitched and giggled. 'Africa, this is Matthew Kesterton.'

'How do you do,' said Chloe. They shook hands. Chloe conquered her giggles and managed to look businesslike for a split second. I was pleased with her. 'We're business partners,' she said, as we sat down. 'Not – uh – lesbians or anything.' God! I was instantly so *not* pleased with her! What an idiotic thing to say. I shot her a furious glance.

'So, Matthew,' I said in the twee tinkling voice of an elf getting down to the serious stuff, 'can you tell us a bit about your previous work experience?'

'Yes,' said Matthew, looking me straight in the eye with a kind of weird confidence. 'I've brought my CV as a matter of fact.' He snapped open his briefcase and pulled out an immaculate piece of paper. He handed it over. It was beautifully set out and printed.

'I've done a bit of everything, really,' said Matthew. 'Care assistant, relief support worker, kitchen assistant, waiter, handyperson, shelf stacker, cleaning operative, part-time receptionist, clerical assistant, warehouse operative.' I tried not to faint. 'And web design, of course,' he added modestly.

'Wow!' said Chloe. 'Amazing!' Matthew gave her a contemptuous look, and turned back to me. That *lesbian* remark had put him right off Chloe. Clearly he had decided that I was the only person present who was not beneath him. He was wrong, though. Now I'd heard what he'd done, I realised I was several thousand miles beneath him. But he must never know.

'I've also got three referees,' said Matthew, fishing another piece of paper out of his bag and handing it over. I glanced down. There were three names and addresses. Boy, was he serious about this job. I felt guilty that we were, in fact, totally wasting his time. But we just had to get on with it.

'So, Matthew, you're obviously very experienced,' I squeaked. He gave a serious little nod. I could see Chloe scratching her cheek. She does this when she's trying not to laugh. My weird tiny voice was freaking her out. 'So . . . which of these jobs did you enjoy most?' Chloe scratched again, and emitted a kind of hysterical gasp, which she tried to disguise as a cough.

'I liked being a receptionist,' said Matthew.

'Because of the responsibility. Dealing with people. Sorting out problems. But I like brainstorming too . . .'

He just talked on and on and on and on about all the lovely work he'd done. No expressions ever crossed his face, and I noticed that his eyes were a curious colour. I wasn't sure what I'd call it. Khaki, possibly. It wasn't a good colour for eyes. Not on planet earth, anyway.

'Problem-solving,' he was saying, in his dull, pasty way. 'Troubleshooting.'

Listen, buddy, I was so tempted to say, *just push off and do your brainstorming and troubleshooting and poodle-fiddling somewhere else, because I'd rather be run over by a cement truck than go to the Ball with you for even a split second.*

'Interesting!' I squeaked with a gracious smile.

'I imagine that's the sort of thing you're looking for?' he asked with a pasty, khaki glare. I was startled for a moment. What *was* I looking for? 'Being a life coach is all about troubleshooting and problem-solving, isn't it?' Matthew informed me.

'Yes, of course, it's an important part of the approach,' I replied, trying to sound as if I knew all there was to know about being a life coach, even though I knew precisely zilch and Matthew clearly knew heaps.

'So how does it work, then, exactly?' asked Matthew. I began to feel as if I was the one being interviewed. Suddenly I broke out in a cold sweat. Two things were wrong.

My first problem was that I had to explain to this robo-boy how exactly our prize-winning business operated – and I hadn't the faintest idea even how to life coach a *flea*.

But the second problem was way, way more serious than the first. I could feel a horrible, painful, squeezing pain spreading through my tum. Oh God! All those baked beans! The moment of reckoning had arrived! The choice before me was simple and stark: either I had to emit a serious of deafening farts, or pass out on the floor from intestinal agony.

11

SUNDAY 2.28 P.M.

A disastrous and disgusting episode

'Just excuse me one moment!' I said, leaping to my feet in what I hoped was an elegant soaring movement worthy of a life coach. 'I think we may have some of those brochures upstairs, Africa!' I walked swiftly from the room.

By some miracle of muscles, I managed to hold my bum shut till I got to Chloe's bedroom. I shut the door behind me, grabbed a cushion (as a kind of silencer) and farted into it. The door flew open. Chloe rushed in.

'What are you *doing*?' she whispered in a hectic rush.

'Shut the door!' I hissed. 'I'm farting! Those goddam beans!' Chloe started giggling. I closed the door and groaned.

'There's another one coming!' I let rip with gusto. 'I'm sorry!'

'Me too!' gasped Chloe, and produced a sound like a fairy trumpet: high-pitched, cute and cheeky. 'Oh my God!' she gasped. 'And this *Africa* stuff! And why are you talking like a freakin' insect? Oh my God! Oh my God!'

She fell on her bed, shaking with hysterical laughter. At the end of every breath she gave a kind of tiny, almost silent scream, as if she was going to suffocate. No way would she be ready to go back down to the interview in a moment or two.

'What . . . are we . . . going to do?' gasped Chloe.

'Never eat beans again!' I whispered. 'Listen . . . I think I'm OK for a minute, now. I'd better go downstairs. I'll say we've both got food poisoning and we'll get back to him later.'

'We can't do that!' said Chloe. 'He'll think we're weird!'

'Who cares?' I shrugged. 'He's a Grade A nerd anyway.'

'I thought he was quite nice!' said Chloe, frowning.

'Listen,' I walked up and down a bit, trying to settle my insides, 'I think the worst of mine is over.

I'll go down and tell him we can't find the brochures, but you're still looking. You come down when you're ready. I'll make up some garbage about being a life coach, and then we'll get rid of him. OK?' Chloe nodded. She needed to fix her face. Her mascara had run.

I went downstairs. Halfway down the stairs I had a nasty fit of silent and helpless giggling again. Horrid. Finally, though, I managed to sober up by thinking of starving children in a desert landscape.

Matthew was leafing through a magazine. He looked up as I entered, but without smiling.

'I'm sorry,' I said. 'We can't find any brochures. They're reprinting. Chl—Africa's just having an extra look round the office. It's chaos up there! We've been so busy!' I made what I thought was a graceful gesture indicating our fabulous success.

'Maybe . . . you need a life coach yourself?' suggested Matthew. He had made a joke, but without showing any signs whatever of amusement. I laughed generously, while realising that deep down in my tummy, more trouble was brewing.

'You're so right!' I said. 'Oh – I forgot – we usually interview people to music. It creates an ambulance, you know.' I went over to Chloe's CD player.

'Ambience, I mean.' I was so flustered, I'd *need* a goddam ambulance if this went on much longer.

I selected a Beethoven CD, inserted it, and pressed PLAY. Beethoven was classy – classic, even, and he was loud. He would cover any unfortunate sounds I might be forced to make. I could always have a coughing fit as well, just to be on the safe side.

But what was this? This was not Beethoven. Literally the worst song in history burst out: *'I'm horny, I'm horny horny horny!'* Matthew looked startled. Chloe entered the room. She hadn't done a very good job of repairing her eye make-up. She looked as if she'd been crying.

'Zoe!' she frowned. 'What's this?'

It just kept on blasting out. *'I'm horny, I'm horny horny horny!'*

'It was in the Beethoven case!' I snapped. 'I wanted to play some Beethoven to create ambience!' I was also really annoyed with her for calling me Zoe when she knew perfectly well I was Squeaky Jane.

'Switch it off! Switch it off!' yelled Chloe, running to the CD player. In her haste she knocked into a framed photo of their dog, Geraint. It flew through the air and smashed into the wall. The glass broke.

Chloe screamed. She turned off the *Horny* song.

There was a sudden silence, in which I farted.

Then Matthew's phone suddenly started to ring. It was the Crazy Frog – I felt his ringtone let him down really. So trashy, and *so* last season. However, I was hardly in a position to look down on Matthew stylewise. I had just farted in his face, and as he answered his phone, I ran out into the garden and farted three more times.

'Good afternoon!' came a man's voice behind me. I turned round. Chloe's neighbour was clipping his hedge and staring disapprovingly at me over his glasses.

'Good afternoon!' I cried. Then I ran indoors. Matthew was on the phone. He had walked over to the window and was staring out into the garden where I'd just been. I glanced hopelessly at Chloe, who was picking up pieces of glass.

I bent down to help her, and farted again. This was the end. I was either going to burst into tears or die laughing. I leapt up, ran upstairs and locked myself in Chloe's bathroom. I turned on all the taps, to make as much noise as possible, wrapped a towel round my head, and howled.

A couple of minutes later, when my panic attack was finished and my body felt nice and quiet again, I turned off the taps. I heard the front door slam shut. He must have gone! I waited. I heard Chloe coming upstairs.

'Zoe!' she shouted. 'It's OK! He's gone! Are you all right?'

I opened the bathroom door. 'What a complete and utter nightmare,' I said. Now he'd gone, the urge to laugh had somehow disappeared.

'His mum rang,' said Chloe. 'There was some crisis at home, so he had to go. I said we'd be in touch.'

'Poor Matthew,' I said. 'He really was trying to have a job interview, and all we could do was fart at him, play obscene music and throw the ornaments about.'

'I thought he was quite nice, really. In a way,' Chloe said. 'I mean, in casual clothes, and you know, if you could get him to loosen up a little . . .' She looked thoughtful.

'Well, thank God he's gone,' I sighed. 'Now we can chill out and enjoy the rest of the afternoon. Let's watch that new Keanu Reeves DVD.' Then suddenly a terrible thought struck me. 'Oh noooo!' I wailed.

Chloe looked alarmed.

'What is it?' she asked. 'What? What?'

'The nightmare's not over,' I informed her. 'Scott Nicholls is coming in a minute.'

Chloe looked blank.

'Who's Scott Nicholls?'

'The other one.'

12

SUNDAY 2.46 P.M.

Worse and worse. And worse.

I reminded Chloe that Scott was the dreamy, poetic one and that he'd probably be loads more romantic than Matthew. He'd probably have wonderful lyrical hazel eyes and long, fine, sensitive hands. His handshake would be warm, firm and lingering.

'Just thinking about him is making my lips tingle,' I assured her, ransacking my make-up bag. I was torn between two lipsticks: Porsche Red and Brandy Ice.

'OK,' said Chloe. 'You've convinced me. I just need to work on my mascara a bit.'

We both fixed our faces, then cleared up the broken glass and polished the coffee table again. Eventually we were ready. Scott was due at 3 p.m. and it was 2.57 p.m. precisely. We sat in our interviewing positions, trying to keep calm.

'If it all goes pear-shaped,' I said, 'you say you're just going to pop to the bathroom, then go upstairs and ring me on my mobile. I'll take the call, and then I'll tell him my dog's been run over or something, so we have to end the interview.'

'Zoe!' cried Chloe, her eyes filling with tears, 'Don't say that! If anything ever happened to Geraint I couldn't bear it!'

'No, no, listen,' I said. 'I didn't mean Geraint. I don't even have a freakin' dog. I was just – oh never mind. Just say *anything*. He won't be able to hear what you say, anyway, will he? I'll just make something up. Don't say anything funny though, or I'll kill you. It's got to be a sudden emergency.'

'So I do this if the interview's gone pear-shaped?' asked Chloe. 'How will I know?'

'Oh, you'll know,' I said grimly.

'OK, listen. If I think you want me to go upstairs and ring you, I'll make a secret sign,' said Chloe. 'Then you have to make a secret sign back.' Sometimes I think Chloe's got a lot of growing up to do.

'OK, OK,' I said rather rattily. 'What's the secret sign?'

'I'll scratch my neck,' said Chloe.

'But you're always scratching your neck.'

'No, I promise I won't unless I want to know if it's gone pear-shaped. Then, if you agree it's gone pear-shaped, you scratch your head.'

'OK,' I said. 'In fact, I'll scratch my head if I think it's gone pear-shaped, whether you've scratched your neck or not.'

'OK,' said Chloe. 'So if I see you scratching your head, and I want to make sure it's because it's gone pear-shaped, I'll scratch my neck, OK?' I was beginning to feel dizzy with conspiracy.

'Uh . . . yes,' I said. BAZZZZZZZ! The doorbell! It was Scott! We both leapt up, panicking. Chloe backed off in the direction of the kitchen and waved me towards the front door.

'Listen,' I said, 'if either of us scratches by accident, we cough, OK? So the cough means: sorry, that was an accident – I scratched myself by mistake. OK?'

'And what if we cough by accident?' said Chloe. I was halfway to the door by now. My mind went blank. 'What's the, like, ultimate code for "*it's gone pear-shaped*"?' hissed Chloe.

'We ask him if he'd like a cup of coffee,' I

whispered, and then ran to the door. I took a deep breath. This time it was going to be fine. Scott would be lovely. I was sure of it. I opened the door and realised in a sickening flash: it had gone pear-shaped already.

The weediest boy in the world stood there. He was skinny, and wearing drainpipe jeans and a gothic T-shirt with the word 'VOMIT' in silver sparkly letters on black. His neck was scrawny. His hair was so short, it was almost shaved. His lips were strangely puffed up and looked too big for his face. His eyes were pale blue and sort of fishy.

'Uh, hi,' he said. 'Is this the right place?' He didn't even introduce himself. What a dingbat.

'Scott?' I enquired, feeling suave and mature – about thirty-five years old. I extended my hand. He kind of flinched, looked panicky, and attempted to shake hands with me – but somehow his hand missed mine and travelled on, up the inside of my arm, dislocating my thumb on the way.

'S-sorry!' said Scott. Good God, the poor guy was incapable of the most basic actions. I wondered whether he'd be able to walk in and sit down, or whether I ought to put him out of his misery and carry him in.

'Come in!' I beamed. I now felt ludicrously mature: about forty-five. Scott lurched forward and entered the house. He did trip on the doormat but I suppose it was a major triumph that he didn't actually fall flat on his face.

I ushered him into the room, and there was a terrible moment when Chloe couldn't hide her shock and disgust at his vile appearance. Her face kind of collapsed into horror, and then tried to climb back into a smile.

'This is Scott Nicholls,' I said. 'Scott, this is Chloe Watson, my business partner. We've taken over the project from Jane and Africa,' I gave Chloe a firm look. There was to be *no* laughing, and no mention of our not being lesbians. Scott would probably die of fright.

'Do sit down,' said Chloe in a strange, nervous headmistressy voice. 'Would you like a cup of coffee?' Then she realised that she'd inadvertently used the code word for '*it's all gone pear-shaped*'. Even though, in some ultimate kind of way, it really *had* gone pear-shaped, it was still far too soon for my dog to be run over.

'Oops!' She gave a kind of convulsive start, and looked at me with frantic apology in her eyes. Scott didn't notice. He was trying to work out how to sit down on the sofa without accidentally killing himself. 'What I really meant was, would you like a cup of *tea or* coffee?!' She said this with a crazy kind of emphasis, so I would know she hadn't meant to use the code.

'Yes, please,' said Scott in a faint, distressed voice. 'Coffee.'

'Milk and sugar?' asked Chloe.

'Yes, please,' said Scott.

'How many sugars?'

Scott hesitated, picking invisible dust off the knees of his trousers. 'Four,' he said.

Chloe looked amazed and disgusted. She scratched her neck. Had she meant to? Had she even noticed she'd done it? 'Would you like some coffee, Zoe?' she asked me.

'Yes, please,' I said, scratching my head to ask if she'd meant to scratch her neck. A terrible light dawned in her eyes.

'Did I scratch my neck just then?' she asked – the *idiot*. She had now blown our entire strategy.

'Yes,' I said, enraged. 'You must try and stop it, Chloe!'

'Sorry,' she said, trying to turn it into a joke. 'It's

just a nervous habit.'

Scott wasn't really listening. He looked if he was already desperate to escape. I picked up my notebook and cracked it open purposefully. Chloe went off to the kitchen to make the coffee. I reached for my pen.

'So – Scott,' I said. 'First things first. What's your name?' Scott looked puzzled. 'Oops! Sorry!' I tried not to look like an idiot. 'Of course, I know your name. Scott . . .' I wrote *Scott* down in my book. Then something terrible happened. *I forgot his surname*. I was so obsessed with scratching or not-scratching, coughing or not-coughing, that everything else had been wiped from my memory banks.

I couldn't help blushing and having a major panic attack kind of in secret. But I really *couldn't* admit I had forgotten his surname. So I pretended to write his surname next to his first name. What I wrote, in fact, was 'Saucepanhead.' He would never see what I had written, of course. He couldn't see my notebook from where he was sitting. He would just see that I'd written *something* and assume it was his surname.

'I mean, of course, what's your address?' I went on, trying to appear relaxed and mature by smiling broadly. Even though the smile was twitching slightly. It was totally synthetic and bogus and longing to drop right off my face.

'Mynydd Mawr,' he said, only it sounded like *Munuth Mauwer*. I panicked slightly.

'Sorry?' I said, pen poised.

'Mynydd Mawr,' he repeated. 'It's – uh, Welsh. My mum's from Wales.'

'How lovely!' I gushed. 'We went camping in Wales once! It rained all the time but it was gorgeous all the same! ... Er, how do you spell it ... ? M, U ...'

'Not U,' said Scott. 'Why not you.'

'*Why not me?*' I repeated, rapidly losing it.

The faintest trace of a grin flashed briefly across Scott's face.

'Y not U,' he said. 'The letter Y. M Y N Y ...' My hand was starting to shake. I couldn't concentrate. And my head was starting to itch. Any minute now I was going to have to scratch my head, whether Chloe was in the room or not.

'I'll write it down for you, if you like,' said Scott, holding out his hand. He wanted my notebook! The notebook in which I'd written his name as 'Scott Saucepanhead.' He must *never* see that! He might think it was some kind of cruel reference to his appearance, not a random word. Although, to be honest, he was way, way more ugly than a saucepan. 'Saucepanhead' was, in his case, almost a kind of compliment.

'No, no, it's fine,' I said, making a charade out of getting it right, 'I'm just being stupid. M Y N Y . . . ?'

'M Y N Y D D,' said Scott. I wrote it down. 'M A W R.'

I finished it. I now felt slightly more in control.

'What does it mean?' I asked.

'Big Mountain,' said Scott.

'Nice,' I nodded approvingly. 'Poetic. Do you ever write poetry, Scott?'

Scott looked frightened. 'No,' he said. 'Is it . . . like, necessary for the job?'

'No, no,' I said. 'I just wondered . . .' Silence fell. My mind had gone blank. If Chloe had been in the room, I'd have scratched my head at her and said, 'Would you like a coffee?' Even if we were already actually drinking some.

Scott was avoiding my eyes. He was fiddling with his trouser knees again. Kind of scratching. Maybe he also had a code, which was: *if it's all going pear-shaped, scratch your knees.* The truth was, it was all so totally pear-shaped, we'd all be scratching away like apes, the moment Chloe came back with the coffee.

The silence deepened. We needed some meaningless small talk. I pride myself on my ability to chat confidently with random strangers (sometimes described by my sister, Tam, as infantile babble) but my mind was so totally blank, I couldn't remember a single word. In English or Welsh.

Scott looked up and raised his eyebrows slightly. His strange fishlike gaze passed nervously across my face and came to rest on my right ear.

'Westlake Avenue,' he said. I blinked, mystified at this random outburst.

'Sorry?' I enquired.

'It's the rest of my address,' said Scott apologetically. He was still trying, in some dim and fumbling way, to have a job interview. I wondered if we'd manage to communicate before one of us died of old age.

13

SUNDAY 3.14 P.M.

The dog that came back from the dead

Chloe suddenly walked through the room and went upstairs. She smiled and said, 'Excuse me,' as she passed us. I heard her go into the bathroom. She turned the taps on – presumably to blot out the sound of her making the call. I assumed she was going to ring me right now. I jolly well hoped so. I had already been interviewing Scott for what felt like two thousand years.

Suddenly, a baby laughed loudly in my handbag. Scott kind of jumped. I admit it is a bizarre ringtone. I grabbed my phone.

'Hi!' I said. 'I can't talk now, I'm afraid – I'm in a meeting.'

'Oh, I'm really sorry,' said a mysterious masculine

voice. 'This is Oliver. I'll ring back later.' Oliver!!! And he hung up on me. These few words kick-started a major crisis in all my internal organs. Stomachs I never knew I had started break-dancing. My kidneys sizzled as if on a barbecue. My tummy started to beat like an African drum. My face turned red, white and blue – I could feel it.

Scott sat opposite, staring at me. At this most inconvenient moment he had found the confidence to look me in the eye. I had lost a chance to talk to Oliver because I was trapped with this moron. And it was all my fault. What was I doing here? What on earth did I imagine I was playing at?

'So . . .' said Scott. 'What does the uh, job, like, involve, exactly?'

The baby laughed again from my handbag. For a crazy moment I thought it might be Oliver again. I grabbed the phone.

'Hello?' I said, in a seductive voice.

'Listen.' It was Chloe. 'Is it too soon to tell you your dog's been run over?'

'No!' I said, with a tragic gasp. I leapt from my sofa and walked over to the window. I turned my back on Scott, to hide my face. 'How did it happen? When? Where?'

'You told me not to say anything funny, so blah blah blah blah, I'm afraid,' said Chloe. In my near-hysterical state I almost found this too hilarious to bear. But I knew I had to concentrate like mad and make it feel real. It was our only chance of getting rid of Scott *immediately* – which incidentally was already way, way too late for comfort.

'No!' I cried operatically. 'No! Oh, how awful! How is he?'

'Dead!' said Chloe. 'No, wait – sorry, I got that wrong. The dog's fine, but the bus is a write-off. Not bad for a chihuahua.'

A burst of laughter snorted out of me, but I disguised it as a sob of anguish.

'In intensive care?' I spluttered. 'Can I come and see him?'

'Yeah,' said Chloe. 'And don't forget the grapes.'

'I'll come right away!' I said, and rang off. I turned to Scott, who was looking worried.

'My dog's been run over,' I said, trying to keep the urge to laugh *firmly* shut in. I grabbed a tissue, covered my face for a moment, and let out a sob of laughter with my face well hidden. Scott stumbled to his feet. He looked deeply upset. We stood around helplessly in the face of my awful loss.

'God! I'm sorry,' he said.

'I'm *so* sorry,' I kind of sobbed. 'He's in intensive care, down at the vet's. I'll have to go there now.'

'Yeah,' said Scott, looking with obvious longing towards the door. 'God! I hope he makes it.'

Then a really weird thing happened. The front door flew open, and Chloe's huge dog, Geraint, came hurtling in. He headed straight for Scott and started sniffing his trousers with horrid familiarity.

'Geraint!' Chloe's mum, Fran, now entered the room, looking, as usual, like some kind of low-budget street entertainer. Several Indian bags hung from her shoulders – some adorned with little mirrors. She was wearing her hair up in a thick grey pineapple pony-tail, and earrings shaped like gigantic red and white toadstools dangled from her ears. 'Geraint! Stop it! Go in your basket!'

Scott was stroking Geraint's head in an attempt to distract him from his jeans.

'It isn't this dog that's been run over,' I explained. 'This is Chloe's dog. It's my dog.'

'Your dog's been run over, Zoe?' cried Fran in horror. 'I didn't even know you had a dog!'

'We've only just got him,' I explained. 'He's only a puppy.' Tears (God help me) appeared in Fran's eyes.

'Oh my God, how tragic!' she lamented. At this point Chloe came charging downstairs. 'Zoe's dog's been run over!' said Fran.

'I know!' said Chloe, dramatically. Of course she didn't know! She'd been upstairs when I'd got the call, hadn't she? Did she never *think*?

The important thing now was to get Scott out of the house.

'I'm so sorry,' I said to Scott. 'I'm going to have to go and see him. He's in intensive care,' I told Chloe's mum. 'Down at the vet's.'

'Oh, which vet? I'll drive you there if you like,' said Fran, with disastrous sympathy. My mind went blank. I didn't have a clue where any vets were. That's how it is when you aren't allowed any pets. The wonderful world of vets – and vet students – is closed to you.

'That one down by the station!' I made flapping gestures. 'Down that side road. The one with the thingummyjig.' Fran looked puzzled. I turned to Scott. He was longing to go: I was longing for him to go, and yet still, somehow, we hadn't managed to get him even anywhere near the sitting-room door.

'I'm so sorry, Scott!' I said, with a brave smile. 'I'll be in touch.'

'Yeah, thanks.' Scott edged sideways towards the door. 'Sorry about . . . it. Bye.' He ducked out of the sitting room and disappeared into the hall. Chloe followed him and we heard them saying goodbye, and the front door shutting behind him.

'Phew!' I said, and slumped back down on to the sofa.

'You must be very shocked, Zoe, love,' said Chloe's mum. 'Would you like a few drops of my Rescue Remedy?'

'No, thanks,' I said faintly. I now had to explain to Fran that it had all been a lie. Chloe entered the room, and as she did so, a strange sound rang out. It was Chloe's latest ringtone – a flamenco chicken.

'Hello?' she said, and then she went red. Instantly I knew it had to be Beast.

'When shall we go to the vet's?' Fran asked me. 'Right away?'

Chloe sped furtively from the room. I could hear her muttering secretly into her mobe as she ran upstairs. Her bedroom door slammed shut. 'Or would you like a cup of tea first?' Fran went on. She was being so nice, so supportive, and yet somehow, I wanted to kill her – in the comfort of her own home, too.

'Fran,' I said heavily, 'I have a huge confession to make. We invented all that about my dog being run over to get rid of that nerdy boy.'

Fran's face creased into a huge smile. 'Ha ha!' she laughed, and clapped her hands. 'Brilliant! No dead dog! No dog fighting for life! Re-sult!' And she waltzed off to the kitchen, chuckling to herself. Though she sometimes uses inappropriately youthful slang, Chloe's mum does have a nice festive kind of character. My mum would have interrogated me for hours, and left me feeling I had committed a dreadful crime.

I was now free to run upstairs and eavesdrop on Chloe's phone call. But as I arrived I heard her saying goodbye. I knocked on the door. She flung it open. Her face was alight with excitement.

'Zoe!' she whispered, pulling me inside. 'Beast's invited us to the Next Big Thing – tonight! It doesn't start till eight! We've got plenty of time to get ready – isn't it amazing?'

'Hang on,' I said. 'We're babysitting tonight, remember?'

'He's absolutely adorable.' Chloe wasn't even listening. She was staring in a dreamy kind of way at the carpet. 'He's not at all like people say. He said I was beautiful.'

I felt a pang of rage. I didn't want Chloe waltzing off to events with boys while I stayed behind, baby-sitting. I was starting to change into a nerd.

In fact, it was happening already. I looked at my feet. They had already become flat and smelly. Soon the nerdhood would spread to the rest of me. I would have to marry Scott and have nerdy babies with strange fishy eyes.

'But the Next Big Thing is only for sixth formers,' I objected.

'He says he can smuggle me in. And you must come too, with Donut.' Suddenly the red mist descended on me.

'Chloe, no!' I exploded. 'I don't want to go to the freakin' sixth-form party with that Neanderthal! We're supposed to be getting ourselves organised for the Earthquake Ball!'

'But that's not for another week!' shouted Chloe. 'The Next Big Thing's tonight! Come on, Zoe, don't front! We're playing Major League now!'

'*Front? Major League?*' I repeated. 'What language are you speaking, pray? Some kind of Beastly slang, presumably? Listen, Chloe, we have to babysit tonight. I can't get out of it, OK?'

'No, no!' said Chloe. Her lower lip started to stick

out and tremble. 'Stuff babysitting! I'm going to the Next Big Thing! I never promised to go babysitting with you. The Normans are your babysitting people, not mine. I'm sorry, Zoe, but if you don't want to go to the Next Big Thing with me, I'll have to go without you.'

Her green eyes kind of flashed. It's not often Chloe challenges me like that. I knew she would never change her mind, so I just flashed my eyes right back and picked up my jacket.

'I'll go, then,' I said. I was seething with fury at the way she'd let me down, but I didn't make a melodramatic exit, slamming her door or anything. I just kind of stalked grandly out of the house.

I was dreading my babysitting torment that evening with the loathsome Norman twins. At times in the past, Chloe had really helped me out, and even though she hadn't actually promised to come and give me some support tonight, she'd kind of gone along with the idea.

But then Beast had rung and summoned her, and she was off. Where was her loyalty to me, her oldest friend, in my hour of need? Gone. I was going to have to face my ordeal alone, while she partied with party animals.

And to top it all, Oliver had rung, and I had somehow managed to hang up on him! Could life possibly get any worse?

That evening I approached the dreaded Norman house. The screaming inside was clearly audible from miles away. The front door was open, as if Mr and Mrs Norman couldn't wait to escape. I hesitated on the doorstep.

'Hello!?' I cried softly, but of course my weedy little call was obliterated by the rumpus within.

However, a moment later Mrs Norman appeared, large and complacent in crumpled linen. Behind her the twins were running round, stark naked and brandishing bananas. Seeing me, they raced to the door.

'Sorry, Zoe,' she said. 'The doorbell's broken.' As if she thought she had to apologise for *that* random detail.

'I've got a big wee-wee!' yelled Ben, flashing his banana. Or possibly it was Jack.

'I've got a bigger wee-wee and I'm going to pee all over Zoeeeee!' screamed Jack, or possibly Ben, pointing his banana menacingly at me. I would remember this later, and marvel at his psychic powers.

Mrs Norman smiled at me as if to say, '*Aren't my twins just the most adorable and witty little fellows on the entire earth?*'

My shoulders heavy with the feeling of imminent doom, I stepped inside.

14

SUNDAY 7.32 P.M.

The worst evening of my life so far

'We might be a bit late back,' said Mrs N above the sound of the twins, who had tired of pretending to pee on me and were now demolishing the kitchen. 'I've made up the bed in the spare room in case you want to stay.'

'Oh, thanks,' I said swiftly, 'but I ought to go home afterwards. It's only a couple of hundred metres and I am nocturnal.' Last time I stayed, the twins had woken me up at 5 a.m. by thrashing my head with a rubber snake. 'Don't worry,' I went on, trying to look capable and serene as plastic beakers whizzed past my head – like a reporter in a war zone – 'I've got loads of homework and when that's done I'll get stuck into a DVD.'

After a bit of messing about, during which time the twins were persuaded into their pyjamas, the adult Normans left. Whenever they wave goodbye I have the horrible illusion that they're never going to come back, ever, and I'm going to have to look after Ben and Jack for the rest of my life. I turned on the terrible twins and tried to look extremely frightening.

'Right!' I squeaked, unfortunately missing the ringing tones of vocal authority I was striving for. 'If you're not upstairs and in bed by the time I've counted ten, there will be No Story!'

The twins ran upstairs, yelling like banshees. But this wasn't progress. They didn't go to their room. They raced to the bathroom. A big sponge was floating in the washbasin. Twin A grabbed it and hurled it at Twin B. His pyjamas were saturated. He screamed. He grabbed a plastic mug and hurled more water over Twin B, who was laughing evilly.

'Stop it!' I roared. I strode forward and pulled the plug out of the washbasin. The twins were fighting behind me now. Which was worse: having them fighting each other or turning their Satanic energies on me? 'Right!' I shouted. 'We're going to have to get you some clean pyjamas. Take your clothes off!'

'Take *your* clothes off!' yelled Twin B.

'Yeah!' shrieked Twin A. 'Show us yer bum!'

They tugged at the belt of my jeans. Thank God I wasn't wearing a skirt. The first time I ever babysat for them, I'd been wearing a skirt, a long flowing one, and they had somehow ended up inside it, informing me that they were on a camping trip. My gran says children should know their place, but I'm sure it shouldn't be actually *inside your clothing*.

'Next time you go to the loo, we want to watch!' shouted Twin B.

'I would rather eat a live rhino,' I informed him crisply.

'I'm a rhino!' screeched Twin A, charging me and head-butting me in the tummy, quite painfully.

'Stop it!' I roared. 'And get those wet pyjamas off!' They both pulled off their PJs and started running around naked again. 'Stand still!' I shouted. 'Or I'll phone the police!' They ignored me. We were back to square one.

I went downstairs. OK, I was abandoning my responsibilities, but frankly I'd already had more than I could stand. I went into the sitting room and picked up my handbag. I was so tempted to ring Mum and ask her to come over. She'd offered. But I wanted to hack it on my own. If only Chloe hadn't let me down by going off to the Next Big Thing, the treacherous bitch.

There was the thunderous noise of the twins coming – or possibly falling – downstairs, and they rushed in.

'Are you going to phone the police?' they asked breathlessly in unison.

'Yes,' I snapped, hastily improvising. I got out my phone, dialled a random number and waited for 'a reply'. It wasn't even ringing, of course. The twins watched, open-mouthed. For a moment there was perfect silence and peace.

'Is that the police station?' I said suddenly. 'Yes, uuuuh, my name's Zoe Morris and I'm babysitting at 32 Prince's Gardens. I've got two boys here, Jack and Ben Norman, and they're completely out of control. Can you send an officer round, please?' Then I waited, and nodded, and said, '*Uh-huh*,' and went through a big charade as if I was getting put through to where the officers are.

'You'll be round in ten minutes?' I said. 'That's brilliant! And are you going to actually arrest them? . . . Oh, really.' I covered up the mouthpiece and looked soberly at the twins. 'The policeman says he'll be able to take you to prison straightaway.'

'It's a trick!' squealed Twin B. For a moment I had had them worried, but suddenly, somehow, the spell was broken.

'What's in your handbag?' Twin A yelled, and dived into my most sacred and private receptacle outside my actual body.

'Get out of my bag, you beast!' I snatched the bag out of his horrid little paws, and everything flew across the room: coins, hankies, cosmetics, tampons, my broken pedometer, my tweezers, the lot. The twins crowed in delight.

'If you're not upstairs and in your bedroom in ten seconds,' I screeched, 'you won't get *The House at Pooh Corner!*' This was their favourite book.

'Poo!' yelled Twin B delightedly.

'Poo!' screamed the other. 'Pee! Bum!' They ran round and round me, yelling out the rudest words they could think of. And somewhere, privately, in the deep recesses of my brain, I flung my rudest words right back. I'm never going to have children. They're just completely pointless.

Eventually they went to sleep. In their own beds, though not wearing pyjamas. I don't know how it happened. They'd tired themselves out, I suppose. They'd certainly completely and utterly exhausted *me*. I lay on the sofa and just enjoyed the total silence for five minutes. Then I started to ransack the Normans' DVD collection.

I found the original 1939 version of *Wuthering Heights* and decided to give it a whirl. It was in black and white and really spooky. I dimmed the lights and noticed that the wind was picking up outside – just right for a romantic romp with the ghosts on the moors.

Quite early in the film, there's a frantic tapping on the window and the ghost of Cathy cries, 'Let me in! Let me in!' Mr Lockwood opens the window and her icy hand grabs his wrist. She won't let go, and in desperation he rubs her hand against the broken glass, trying to shake off those madly clutching fingers. I watched in terror.

Then, moments later, there was a tapping at my window! Right *here* in the real world! And the wind was howling now, literally *wuthering* around the house. My blood ran cold. I hid under a throw. The tapping at the window increased.

'Let me in! Let me in!' Oh God, this was a bad dream. I was being haunted. The film had come to life. Or maybe I had gone into the film. 'Let me in! Let me in!' the high voice wailed above the storm.

There was a clap of thunder. My heart was pounding so hard, my ribs were on the point of exploding.

'Let me in! Zoe! Let me in!' Wait. The voice knew my *name*? I tiptoed to the window. My legs felt weak and shaky. Gingerly I opened the curtains a tiny crack, and looked out. There, soaking wet and lit up by the eerie light of the distant streetlamps, stood Chloe.

'Open the freakin' door!' she yelled. 'Let me in! The goddam doorbell's broken!'

I raced to the front door and opened it. Chloe kind of fell in, panting, dripping, and, I'm sorry to say, sobbing.

'It's a nightmare!' she gasped, gripping my arm with icy, ghostly fingers. 'My life is technically over!'

15

SUNDAY 9.45 P.M.

Life is a horror movie . . .

'It was a total disaster!' cried Chloe, falling into my arms. I just hugged her till she stopped sobbing, even though she was sopping wet. Sometimes a major hug is required no matter what. When she'd stopped crying I led her to the sofa and found a towel for her hair. I was scared she had caught a chill or something. She was sort of shaking madly and her teeth were chattering.

'I was at the Next Big Thing,' she said in a shivery voice, 'and this girl turned up, and was like, *"Who the hell do you think you are?"* And she started shouting and stuff about me not being a sixth former, but she was having a go at Beast really, you could tell, and the thing was, I think she thought she was going out with him, so she was like *mad with jealous rage.*'

'Hmm, pants!' I said sympathetically. 'I'm going to make you a hot chocolate.'

'Wait! I haven't finished!' Chloe clutched at my arm, and she felt just like the icy cold ghost of Cathy. 'At first I thought she was just, like, in a strop, then I could see she was jealous of me being with Beast, but *then* she just kind of flew at me, and I realised she was *drunk.* She pulled my hair and kicked me and all sorts of mad stuff. Beast tried to reason with her and they pulled her off me, but I just ran. I ran and ran and ran to your house, and your mum told me you were here.'

'OK,' I said. 'Listen. I'm going to be very boring now. I want you to go upstairs and have a hot shower. I'll put your clothes in the tumble-dryer. You can wear Jackie's dressing gown till your clothes are dry again. And I'll make you that hot choc. And then you can tell me all about it again, in slow-motion action replay.'

'Th-thanks, Zoe. Thanks,' said Chloe, still shivering. She didn't smile, but she had finished crying. I could tell.

'And for God's sake, don't wake the twins,' I said.

Soon my maternal plan was serenely in progress.

Chloe was warm and cosy in Jackie Norman's red velour dressing gown, her clothes were tumbling dry, and we were both sipping hot choc and trying to get back into *Wuthering Heights*.

'I tried to read *Wuthering Heights* once,' said Chloe, 'but there were too many people called Cathy in it.' I was relieved she was talking about something else apart from what a two-timing heart-breaking cad Beast was. Then there was a knock at the window and a shout outside – a masculine voice this time.

'Oi!' it said. 'Open up!'

'Who the hell's that?' I muttered, getting up and going to the window. I peeped through the curtains. Oh no!

'It's Beast and Donut!' I gasped. 'And another bloke who looks like a weasel!'

'Don't let them in!' screeched Chloe, cowering feebly inside her dressing gown. I made Go Away gestures, but the guys just kept on yelling.

'Open the door! The doorbell's bust!'

'I'll just go and tell them to clear off,' I said. 'You stay here!'

I opened the front door, but unfortunately the Normans didn't have a chain, so Beast, Donut and the weaselly person just kind of bundled in past me.

'Stop!' I yelled. 'Nobody said you could come in!'

'Where's Chloe?' demanded Beast, looking round. 'Chloe!' he bawled at the top of his voice.

'Shhhh!' I hissed. 'You'll wake the twins! – Chloe's not here – oh!'

Chloe had appeared in the sitting room doorway. She looked absolutely furious.

'You've got a nerve!' she shouted. Just occasionally, when she's totally fired up, Chloe can yell for England. 'Asking me to the party when you'd already asked somebody else! How humiliating was that! Can you imagine – can you *imagine* how I felt when that girl started wrestling with me, for God's sake? In front of the entire sixth form? What the hell were you playing at? It was a nightmare! I never want to see you or speak to you again!'

'Sssssh!' I whispered. 'The twins!'

'You look fabulous in that dressing gown, babe,' said Beast, grinning evilly at Chloe. 'Red is definitely your colour! And you're so beautiful when you're angry!' The two other guys laughed. I turned on them.

'What,' I demanded, 'are you two doing here anyway? This is nothing to do with you! And how did you find your way here?' I felt indignant about so many things, I didn't know where to begin.

'He rang Chloe's mum,' said Donut, 'and she gave us your phone number, and your dad said you were babysitting here.'

'Listen, babe,' said Beast, cocking his head on one side and approaching Chloe, 'I know you're mad at me. That girl is insane, though. She's obsessed. She means nothing to me. She's just my kind of – uh, stalker.' The other guys laughed. Chloe backed off towards the kitchen.

'I don't care!' she yelled. 'I DO NOT CARE! Go away! Do you understand English? GO AWAY!' She was starting to shake again.

Suddenly, disastrously, there was a wakeful wail from upstairs. Then the other one joined in. My blood ran cold. This was more terrifying than *Wuthering Heights*. More terrifying than the relentless cold-bloodedness of the Beast seduction technique. The twins had woken up!

'Waaaaaaaaaagh!' came one cry.

'Waaaaaaaaaagh!' came another.

Moments later they were standing at the top of the stairs, stark naked and whingeing for England in stereo.

'God!' said Beast. 'Don't point that thing at me!'

But it was too late.

'Wanna wee-wee!' wailed one twin, and disastrously, started to pee right there and then, in a horrid golden arc, right down the stairs and on to the guests and the very expensive carpet.

'Stop!' I yelled. 'Jack! Ben! Go to the bathroom!'

Foolishly, I blundered forward and tried to rush upstairs without getting peed on. Mission impossible. Before I was halfway up the other twin had started to pee too. They were like dogs marking out territory. And I was the territory.

The guys down in the hall were cracking up, helpless with glee. And Chloe was still yelling at Beast, yelling at the top of her voice.

'Go away!' she screeched. 'Don't you understand plain English? GO AWAY!' It was, in a word, pandemonium.

And it was at this moment that the front door opened and Mr and Mrs Norman stepped inside. They aren't usually cross sort of people. In fact, if they had got cross with their own brats more often right from the start, the world would be a much more gracious place. Their inability to get cross or yell at their offspring was legendary. But this was different.

Their hall was full of large young men they'd

never met before. One looked like a weasel, one like a pickpocket and one like an enormous and tasteless root vegetable. A random girl, naked except for Mrs Norman's best velour dressing gown, cowered in the background. And the babysitter from hell (me) was halfway up the stairs, being urinated on by their entirely nude and grouchy children.

'What the hell is going on?' demanded Mr Norman. He doesn't normally say much, which made his present anger all the more alarming. As the official babysitter, I felt it was my duty to explain. Their children's pee was on my head. Normally this would have entitled me to some kind of apology, but I had the feeling that, in the present circumstances, it was just somehow further proof of my total incompetence.

'I'm sorry,' I said. It seemed the best place to start.

16

SUNDAY 11.18 P.M.

A daring escape . . .

'You know Chloe . . .' I faltered. 'She came to babysit with me last time.'

'Sorry about the dressing gown,' said Chloe. You could see she was tempted to take it off guiltily, but that would have increased the number of nude people present to three. Mrs Norman wasn't listening anyway. She was halfway up the stairs.

'They're sleepwalking again,' she said. 'The twins stared down at her like two statues. They had finished peeing now. 'Get the carpet shampoo, Clive,' she said. Mr Norman walked past us towards the kitchen. Mrs Norman hustled the twins off to the bathroom.

'These guys were just leaving,' I said to nobody in particular.

'My clothes must be dry by now,' said Chloe hurriedly. The tumble-dryer was out in the utility room, beyond the kitchen. 'You go and get them!' she whispered to me. She didn't want to tangle with Mr Norman in the kitchen. I pushed past Donut, pausing only to hiss, 'Get lost!' to the guys.

Mr Norman was on his knees, ransacking the cupboard under the kitchen sink.

I tiptoed to the utility room and got Chloe's clothes out of the tumble-dryer. She locked herself in the downstairs cloakroom to get changed. Beast hung about outside, whispering things through the door. I had to leave her to look after herself – there was other stuff to do.

Donut and Weasel were still hanging about in the hall, watching Mr Norman shampooing the stair carpet and sniggering unpleasantly.

'For God's sake!' I whispered. 'Get lost, can't you? Just GO!'

Couldn't they feel the atmosphere of embarrassment that hung heavy on the air? Weasel looked at Donut, shrugged and moved towards the door.

'I'll wait outside, then,' he muttered.

'You too!' I insisted, pushing Donut towards the door.

'We'll wait in the car, yeah?' Donut called to Beast.

'Right!' answered Beast. 'We'll be with you in half a second.'

We? I thought. *Who's he trying to kid?* Moments later, though, Chloe emerged, back in her own clothes and carrying Mrs Norman's dressing gown, which she hung on the hall stand. It looked wrong there, but I could understand that she wouldn't want to take it upstairs with Mrs Norman on the warpath up there.

'OK, Chloe, babe,' said Beast. 'Let's go.'

I turned in disbelief to Chloe. Earlier that evening she had said Beast was a complete and utter cad, and she never wanted to speak to him again. Only moments ago she'd been screaming at him. But it seemed all he had to do was whisper a few sweet nothings, and she was in his power once again. Even now she was following him to the door.

'Chloe!' I gasped. 'I thought you were going to come back to my place!'

'Oh, it's OK, Zoe,' she said. 'The guys will give me a lift home. School tomorrow, yeah? Got to get an early night.' And off they went.

I didn't have much time to be flabbergasted. Mrs

Norman was coming down the stairs, squeezing past Mr Norman, who was shampooing the stair carpet with a resigned expression on his face.

'That's got them back to bed,' she said, staring accusingly at me. 'I must admit I was surprised, Zoe, when we arrived back, to find the house full of people and the twins running around naked.'

I could have said so much in self-defence. But I suddenly realised it was my chance to get out of babysitting for ever. I need never wrestle and struggle with these nasty little oiks, ever again.

'You're absolutely right,' I said. 'I'm terribly sorry. It all went pear-shaped. In your position, I wouldn't feel I could trust me ever again.'

'Oh, I wouldn't go so far as to . . .'

'Yes,' I said firmly. 'It was a disaster. I'm sorry. I admit it. I can't control your children and I feel I should leave it to somebody who can.' I shot her an accusing glance here, because we both knew that thanks to her maternal incompetence, she couldn't control them either. In fact, who could?

'No, no, Zoe, the twins adore you!' said Mrs Norman. She was on the back foot now. I had taken the initiative good and proper. It was a moment of triumph, pretending to be totally useless. I made a mental note to use it again, when I next needed an escape.

'No, it's been a disaster. Excuse me,' I said, and dived into the sitting room to pick up my jacket. Mrs Norman followed me in.

'Zoe, please don't be upset . . .'

'I am upset,' I said. I was becoming upset, actually. Yes! I really was upset. My chin actually trembled. I could feel it go. 'I've made a mess of it here and I don't think it makes sense for me to babysit for you any more. Sorry.'

I walked to the front door. Mrs Norman raced after me, tugging at my sleeve and pleading.

'Oh please, Zoe! Don't say that! I don't mind you having friends over! Of course not – just as long as you tell us first.'

'I didn't know they were going to come over,' I said with what I hoped was simple saintliness. 'I didn't even know Chloe was coming. She just turned up, soaking wet – and the guys were looking for Chloe. It was nothing to do with me. But anyway, thanks a lot! Bye!'

I opened the door and strode out. I had rarely felt so terrific. Mrs Norman stood on the doorstep and actually wailed at my retreating back.

'Zoe!' she cried. 'Wait! Don't leave us like this!'

I turned by the gate and gave her a sad-but-plucky little wave. I also shrugged in a picturesque way. In the film of my life I would be played by Audrey Tatou. Although she'd have to put a bit of weight on first.

Soon I was comfortably out of sight of the Norman house. Mrs N had given up and, I suspect, was even now taking it out on Clive with a series of vicious kicks.

My mobile rang. It was Tam. Darling Tamsin! In the film of my life she would be played by Kate Winslet.

'Tam!' I cried. 'How are you? Where are you? Are you feeling better?'

'I'm in my room,' said Tamsin. 'I haven't slept or eaten for two days. I'm seriously in danger of losing it.'

'Well, at least you're not at the bottom of the river!' I joked, trying to jolly her along.

'I'd never drown myself,' said Tamsin scornfully. 'When you drown your body sort of all swells up.'

'Gross!' I cried. 'You wouldn't want to look fat, would you, even if you were dead.'

There was silence at the other end. I hoped

Tamsin wasn't trying to work out a more stylish way of committing suicide.

'Can't you come up and see me?' asked Tamsin. 'Come tomorrow. Please, Zoe. I need you. You can sleep on my floor. No, I'll sleep on the floor, you can have my bed.'

'But tomorrow's Monday,' I said. 'I've got to go to school.'

'Bunk off,' suggested Tamsin. 'I did it all the time. Tell Mum and Dad you're staying at Chloe's. Just one night, Zoe. It's only an hour on the train. You always make me laugh. Come on, Zoe, PLEASE! I'm in total panic.'

'What's the problem, Tamsin?'

'I'll tell you when you arrive.'

'Promise me you're not pregnant!'

'God, Zoe – what do you think I am, an idiot? Just get your arse over here tomorrow and you can help get me out of this mess.'

'Are you sure you don't want to talk to Mum and Dad about it?'

'If you so much as *mention* the merest *hint of a hint of a hint* of this to Mum and Dad, I shall have to kill you. Sadly.'

It seemed I was going to have to go up to uni

rather sooner than expected – in secret and possibly, in disguise.

'OK,' I said. 'I'll do it. But if I'm found out and get suspended from school and grounded at home, you'll be responsible.'

'Oh never mind all that!' said Tamsin. 'Just come!'

I promised her I would, and rang off. I was nearly home now. I was actually going up my garden path when I realised the Normans hadn't paid me. I had flounced off without a penny. So how was I going to afford the train fare? My Holiday in Newquay Money was asleep in my post office account. It looked as if a little light burglary might be necessary.

17

SUNDAY 11.31 P.M.

Ghastly interrogation

'How was babysitting?' beamed Mum, looking up from an old episode of *The X Files*.

'Oh, fine!' I said airily. 'The twins peed on my head, though, so I'm off to have a shower.'

'How disgusting!' said Mum savagely. 'Those children are completely feral. That woman's a disgrace. I hope she paid you extra.'

'Yeah, fine – see you in a min!' I called, and ran upstairs. I didn't want to get into too much detail about the babysitting fiasco. I didn't feel it had been a total triumph on my part, somehow.

In the shower I made my plans. I would hide some ordinary clothes in my schoolbag. I would set off for school as usual in the morning, but I'd get off the bus three stops early, at the station. I'd go into the ladies' loos and change out of school uniform. And I'd jump on the next train out of town, like something in a spy thriller.

I wrapped my newly fragrant head in a towel, dived into my dressing gown and, in the privacy of my bedroom, I flipped open my laptop and went online to check train times. There was a train at 9.15 a.m., which meant I could be with Tamsin by 10.30 a.m. There was still the little problem of paying for the ticket, though.

There were two possible sources of cash. One was an old teapot with a broken spout. It sits on the kitchen dresser and random coins are put in it from time to time. It might amount to about £20, but if nobody had ransacked it recently it might amount to anything approaching £50. I went downstairs and peered into the teapot: 30p! Not even enough for a packet of peanuts!

The other source of cash was Mum's handbag. It sat nearby on a kitchen chair. It was open and the wallet was peeping cheekily out as if to say, '*Rob me, rob me, go on, you know you want to.*'

I felt sick at the thought of stealing from Mum. She was only in the next room, watching TV. Dad was upstairs, chained to his PC. Stealthily and guiltily I lifted the wallet out of the bag. I thought I'd just check how much was there. If there were loads and loads of notes, she might not miss one or two. I'd only borrow them, of course. I'd collect my babysitting money in a day or two and pay Mum back before she even noticed anything was missing.

I unfastened the wallet and what did I see? A photo of myself, grinning out at me. And a specimen of my signature. It said 'Love you totally and hugely, Mum – always, Zoe.' It had been on my Mother's Day card to her. She'd photocopied it (so as not to wreck the card) and put it in her wallet. There was a photo of Tamsin in there too, but no tender message. Ha! I'd got one over on the glamorous firstborn for once!

I was so deeply touched by my own message of love to Mum that I couldn't complete my daring burglary. What a disaster! Then I had an idea. I heard the finishing music from the TV news and I knew Mum would now emerge for her nightly fix: a cup of something called chai, a sort of milky tea with spices.

I put the kettle on. When Mum emerged, she looked bleary-eyed and sad. It was The News. I don't know why she watches the stuff. It was my job to cheer her up and simultaneously get some money off her. And if I could succeed with Mum, maybe it would turn into a possible career option.

'Chai, Mum?' I enquired, giving her a hug. 'The kettle's on.' These words alone can charm the average adult and lower their blood pressure to a comfortable level.

'Lovely, darling,' she said, sounding tired.

'Guess what!' I said, embarking on an outrageous lie. 'There's a school trip to Stratford-on-Avon in a couple of weeks!'

'Is there?' Mum sounded pleased. 'I don't remember the note about it.'

'You know me. I always lose notes home,' I said, keeping my back turned and getting out the mugs so she couldn't see my face. Sometimes Mum can tell when I'm lying. It's to do with her career in insurance. Once she followed her instincts and identified a man who had deliberately burned down his own home in order to collect the insurance. She said she knew he was guilty because of his body language. He kept touching his nose, apparently.

I had to be very careful not to touch my nose. It started to itch insanely. A thousand invisible ants were running over it.

'It's £35,' I said quickly. 'For the trip – the theatre seat and the bus and everything. Do you want extra cinnamon?' Skilfully I distracted her from details of the trip to her favourite spice.

'What play are you going to see?' she asked.

I panicked. My mind went blank. The only play I could think of was *Twelfth Night* because that was what we saw last time we'd been on a school trip to Stratford. That had been only last term. We couldn't be going to see it *again*. I pretended not to be able to find the cinnamon, ransacking whole cupboards even though I could see it right there in front of me, next to the bread bin.

'Cinnamon, cinnamon, cinnamon . . .' I muttered, on my knees now among the saucepans.

'It's next to the breadbin, Zoe,' said Mum with a sigh. 'What play is it?'

Still harping on the goddam play. My brain literally refused to come up with a single Shakespeare play, even though if I'd been quietly lying on my bed and staring at the ceiling, I could have thought of dozens. Millions, in fact.

'It's thingummyjig,' I said. 'The one with the . . . ghost thing.'

'*Hamlet*?' asked Mum.

151

'*Hamlet*, yes!' I cried.

'Who's in it?' asked Mum, horribly interested. You could tell she was on the point of booking up to see it herself. 'It's my favourite Shakespeare play.' Whoops! I had selected the wrong one. Mum was now simply *too* intrigued by far. If only I'd said we were going to see *The Very Dull History of Duke Boreo of Venice*.

'Who's in it?' I repeated in an offhand way, fiddling with the cinnamon. I wondered whether, if I sniffed the cinnamon, it would stimulate my brain. Or maybe I could sniff it and stage a terrible sneezing and coughing fit which would force Mum to think about something different from Shakespeare. However, I didn't think I could perform well enough to get away with it. Then suddenly I realised I didn't *have* to know who was in the play.

'I don't know,' I said, telling the truth. Although it wasn't *totally* telling the truth in the sense that we were talking about a production which didn't actually exist.

'Tell you what,' said Mum, looking suddenly energised in a quite revolting way, 'let's go and look it up on the RSC's website.'

And leaving her steaming cup of chai to cool on

the table, she headed for the PC. Dad was just winding up and was more than happy to vacate the computer chair. My heart was hammering wildly. Within seconds Mum would discover that there wasn't a production of *Hamlet* in the Royal Shakespeare Company's current schedule. What then?

She logged on to the RSC's website. I felt sick. What should I do? Admit it was a con to try and get money out of her? Never in a million years! Pretend to be muddled and extremely stupid? Certainly. That was always my only hope.

'Yes! There it is!' cried Mum in excitement, navigating the RSC's website. '*Hamlet*!' My heart turned a somersault. Could it be that I had not told a lie after all? You mean there actually was a production of *Hamlet*? Result!

Oh, thank you, thank you, you lovely guardian angel, I prayed silently. What on earth had I done to deserve such divine support?

'My God!' exclaimed Mum. 'How extraordinary! How fascinating! It's an *all-male* production – in *Russian*! I can't wait to hear all about it, Zoe. In fact, I've half a mind to buy a ticket, myself!'

It seemed my prayer of thanks to my guardian

angel had been a little premature. It seemed I was in deep, and possibly also hot, water – right up to my neck. How could it be so difficult just to get my hands on a train fare?

18

SUNDAY 11.58 P.M.

Secret plans for a desperate journey . . .

'Oh, what a shame,' said Mum. 'They've sold out. How clever of Mr Fothergill to book early. I must congratulate him when I see him.'

I made silent plans to keep Mum and Mr Fothergill separate for the rest of their lives. It was kind of the opposite of a dating agency.

'So,' I said, trying not to sound too scheming or grasping, 'can I have the £35, please?'

'Of course you can!' beamed Mum. She logged off (with regret) from the RSC website. We went downstairs and she handed over the loot. 'In fact,' she said, 'you can have an extra £5 for ice creams and coffees and things.' You could see she was really proud of me, going to see an all-male production of *Hamlet* in

Russian. I was going to have to lie for England when I told her all about the 'visit'. And possibly lie for Russia, too.

Still, at least I had the train fare. OK, I had behaved abominably and lied till my face was a tasteful shade of duck-egg blue, but it was all for a good cause. Tomorrow I could bunk off school and go and see Tamsin – and rescue her from whatever dragon it was who had tied her to that rock.

Before I switched off my bedside light, I tried to call Chloe. Her mobile was switched to voicemail. So I whizzed off a text: **HAVE TO DISAPPEAR FOR 2 DAYS PLS TELL MY M&D I AM STAYING WITH YOU TOMORO NIGHT IF THEY ASK.** I was planning to ring my folks tomorrow afternoon – preferably when my dad would be out walking the neighbour's dog between two and three precisely – and leave a message saying I was staying overnight at Chloe's to avoid being interrogated.

In other words, the lying and deception over *Hamlet* was as nothing to the terrors of truanting. I was so scared I could barely eat breakfast. Luckily Mum didn't notice, as she was getting ready to shoot off to a big insurance meeting. By car, thank God. How awful it would have been if she'd been travelling

by train, and as I lurked furtively on the station platform, Mum had suddenly appeared opposite, with
her briefcase and steely glare – and turned that steely
glare on me.

A casual sweatshirt, baseball cap and trainers were
all that was needed to turn my school uniform into
some kind of nerdy travelling outfit. I was hoping to
hide my face with the baseball cap. I'd got shades as
well. I got changed in the station loo as planned, and
stared at myself in dismay in the mirror. I looked like
some kind of transsexual, colour-blind golfing junkie
with a great-grandparent who had been a chim-
panzee.

If only I'd been able to pack a fabulous chic scarlet
and black New York actress outfit with high heels and
a hat the size of a pizza. But I could only pack stuff
that would fit into my school bag. To be honest, I'd
have looked more stylish if I'd stayed in school
uniform.

Never mind. I walked out on to the platform. Oh
no! To my extreme and total horror, Mr Norman was
standing opposite! Looking immensely relaxed and
happy, as you would if you were looking forward to a
blissful day spent miles away from the homicidal
twins you had inadvertently fathered. I was wearing

my baseball cap and shades, but he still clocked me. I could tell he was trying to decide if he recognised me or not. I turned away and walked with a strange hunchbacked shambling motion towards the timetables on the wall.

I could feel Mr Norman's eyes boring into my back. Well, into my backpack. I tried hard to radiate the personality of a shambling hunchbacked transsexual golfing junkie. It wasn't easy.

I heard the sound of teetering high heels totter past behind me. Some kind of sex vision in blonde and black had been sent by my guardian angel to distract Mr N. I could see the whole scene reflected in the glass of the timetable display case. The blonde minced on down the platform, and Mr N (and most of the other men) followed her with their eyes on stalks.

Hoorah! My train was arriving. I made a mental note always to have a blonde stashed away in my luggage. Then if I needed to be particularly incognito, I could let her out, a bit like a cat out of a carrying basket, and she could swank about, fascinating everybody while I furtively got on with the serious business of life.

There was a seat at the far end of the train compartment, kind of tucked away, and I sat down there with my cap pulled well down over my face and read *Heat* magazine. The guard checked my ticket and nodded grimly. He had a face like those mountains carved to look like various US presidents, only a lot less friendly. I bet he would have smiled if I'd been a blonde in black.

Eventually we arrived. I jumped down on to the platform and immediately saw Tamsin waiting for me. She looked just *fabulous*. Excuse me for a few years while I describe her outfit. It started up top with a wonderful sort of fascinator thing with fuchsia feathers on her head.

Her face, was, as usual, beyond beautiful. She looked a bit pale and anxious, but that only added to her charm. Tamsin's face is made for melodrama. She does good tragedy. When my face is sad, I look like a very stale cheese sandwich. She's dramatic. She's a legend. And those cheekbones! Her mum could have been Madonna.

Her jacket was small and black, with a nipped-in waist and jet beading on the lapel. One of her vintage collection. Then there was her dress. It was sublime. It kind of billowed. It was silk, with a pattern of pink strawberries and black and grey leaves. Her shoes were high-heeled, black and drop-dead elegant. Her bag was to die for.

I bounded towards her like a wacky chimp in a tea advert. I felt thrilled and proud that she was my sister, but simultaneously ashamed that I was dressed like a sporty Neanderthal. Tamsin didn't seem to notice, though. She sort of collapsed into our hug like somebody falling downstairs.

Luckily I was feeling particularly strong and chunky, and as we linked arms and walked out of the station she still seemed to be leaning quite heavily on me. Was she ill? Drunk? Or was it just the shoes?

'There's the bus,' said Tamsin, and we crossed the road and got on. We paid our fares and sat downstairs. Tamsin held on tight to my arm. 'Thank you *so much* for coming,' she said. She sighed.

'So what's the problem, then, Tam?' I asked cheerily. I was trying to look as if I could sort anything out, no problem. Unwanted pregnancy? I could arrange for it to be adopted by a film star. Men behaving badly? I could put them in their place with a single flash of my terrible eyes.

'Not on the bus,' whispered Tamsin. She looked around furtively. What did she need to look furtive about? I was the one who was bunking off school. In

160

fact – oh God, I'd almost forgot! If I was going to stay the night here with Tamsin, I *must remember* to ring home and tell them I was staying over at Chloe's.

I hoped and prayed they would be cool about my 'staying over at Chloe's'. We didn't often stay over on weekdays. I'd have to tell them we were working on something. I know! I'd tell them we were working on an assembly.

Oh God! I'd also have to get in touch with Chloe and make sure she'd got my text and was all set to back me up. '*Please, GA,*' I whispered to my sadly overworked guardian angel, '*don't let my parents ring Chloe's landline for any reason.*' The rest of my day was balanced on a high wire of deception. And Tamsin thought *she'd* got problems.

We got off the bus in the town centre and walked a few hundred metres to Waveney Wessex College. Tamsin's room is up on the top floor. I hadn't been there since the previous term. I could hardly believe my eyes. Her room had had the mother of all makeovers.

The bed was covered with a lustrous ruby and silver throw, and there was a huge lamp made out of a Chinese jar. A vast bunch of lilies exploded from a clear glass vase the size of a wardrobe, their heavy scent suggesting a five-star hotel by a Swiss lake or something.

A mobile depicting wacky Victorian gentlemen riding old-fashioned bicycles whirled and turned above the bed. (Frankly, I thought Tamsin's taste had slipped slightly when it came to the mobile, but let that pass.)

One whole wall was covered with the most enormous blow-up picture of Marlene Dietrich, Tamsin's major icon from the era of early cinema. I think Marlene's legs were even longer in this picture than life size. Hanging from a hatstand by the door was a collection of beautiful hats and scarves, many glittering with sequins.

'Wow,' I gasped. 'This is amaaaaaazing, Tam! It's totally fantastic! I adore it!' Tamsin pulled a funny kind of face, kicked off her shoes and filled the kettle at her washbasin. 'And you look fabulous, too. These shoes!' I picked one up and cradled it as one might hold a holy relic. 'They are pure, pure Hollywood. Or do I mean Paris?'

Tamsin said nothing. She switched on the kettle, turned to me, gave a weird, downbeat little shrug and said 'Tea or coffee? Or instant hot chocolate?'

'Whatever you're having,' I said.

'I'm drinking jasmine tea at the moment,' said Tamsin, reaching for an exquisite little teapot on the shelf.

'Jasmine tea?' I had just about heard of it.

'It has flowers in it,' said Tamsin, handing me a packet of loose tea. I sniffed it. It smelt mysterious and grand. Little dried flowers lay sleeping among the tea leaves.

'My God, Tam, you live like a freakin' princess these days,' I said with a broad grin. 'How can anything be wrong when you have this kind of lifestyle?'

'I'll tell you,' said Tamsin. And she went kind of extra, *extra* pale.

19

MONDAY 10.55 A.M.

The moment of truth . . .

'The thing is . . .' Tamsin began. Then my mobile rang. My heart leapt. It was bound to be trouble. Had my truancy been rumbled already? The phone's caller ID said CHLOE, thank God.

'Chloe!' I said, almost shaking with nerves. 'Whassup?'

'Where are you?' asked Chloe. She sounded frantic with worry. I could hear the noise of school mid-morning break in the background, like a riot in the zoo. 'Are you ill or something?'

My heart missed a beat. I had totally forgotten that if somebody's absent, and there's no call from a parent explaining why, the school will ring home and check. This is all because some girl was abducted on the way to school or something really scary. I know it's for our own protection but it's a complete pain.

I had to ring the school NOW and pretend to be my mum. No, wait! I could get Tamsin to do it. But first I had to deal with Chloe, and fast.

'No, listen, I'm with Tamsin.'

'Tamsin? What? At uni?'

'Yeah. Just for the one night, OK? Listen, Chloe, you've got to do something for me. My parents are gonna think I'm staying over with you.'

'But I've told my parents I'm staying over with you!' wailed Chloe.

'Why?' I was outraged. Here I was on a mercy mission to my suffering if well-dressed sister, and instead of offering support Chloe was making frivolous demands.

'It's just something I have to do,' said Chloe. 'It's an overnight thing and it's massively important. I'll explain when I see you.'

I just knew it had something to do with Beast. Oh God! I hoped she wasn't doing anything so rank and tasteless as hopping into bed with him.

'Why have you gone to see Tamsin?' demanded Chloe irritably.

'I'll tell you when I see you,' I replied snappily. 'Well, if *you've* said you're going to be staying over at *my* place, and *I've* said I'm going to be at *your* place, let's hope there aren't any sudden crises or we'll be in big trouble. I just hope whatever adventure you've got in mind is worth it.'

'Don't be so horrible!' cried Chloe. 'You have *no idea* what I'm doing.'

'It's something to do with Beast Hawkins, that much is obvious,' I said. 'All I can say is, you seem to have entirely lost it since you fell under his spell.'

'Shut up, Zoe, you're talking total rubbish! You know nothing! OK? Nothing!' And Chloe rang off with panache.

We've had loads of rows over the years, of course, so normally I would only have been mildly upset. But in my present perilous situation I was terrified. I so needed Chloe on my side, making excuses for me and stitching, if necessary, whole tapestries of inspired lies.

'Quick!' I said to Tamsin. 'I forgot to ring school to say I was ill. You do it – pretend to be Mum.' I dialled the school number and handed the phone over. Tamsin tried to wave it away, and kind of panicked in a thousand different ways, like a demented wind-up clockwork student, but I thrust the phone into her hand.

'Oh, hi . . .' she said in a relaxed drawl, just like Mum when she's got other things on her mind, 'errrrm, this is Mrs Morris, I'm Zoe Morris's mother. Sorry I didn't ring earlier, I'm on a business trip today – uhhh, Zoe's not well today – she's got a tummy bug, so she's staying at home. My husband's looking after her. He works at home, thank God! Keep them in their place! Ha ha!'

She listened for a moment, said her goodbyes, then rang off. My heart was pounding away like a steam hammer – although I'm not sure exactly what a steam hammer is. Basically it was hammering and I was steaming.

'What did they say?' I stammered. 'I was so sure they were going to say they'd already rung home and Dad had said I'd gone to school as usual, and half the police force of England was already searching for me.'

'Well, of course, they did say that,' said Tamsin, stirring the jasmine tea. 'But I soon put them right.'

'Do you realise what I'm going through, coming to see you like this?' I said. I was a bit annoyed that Tamsin had made a joke of it. 'Truanting, having a row with Chloe . . . and if Mum and Dad ever find out, I'm dead on a plate with tomato sauce.'

'Zoe, you are an angel of mercy,' said Tamsin, pouring the tea. 'And I just know you're going to get me out of this jam.'

'What jam?' I asked, feeling suddenly hungry. I'd been too nervous to eat breakfast and now my tummy suddenly went WORRAWORRAWORRAWORRA just like Tigger in *The House at Pooh Corner*. 'Can I have some toast? I'm starving.'

'Just let me fill you in first,' said Tamsin. She sat forward and kind of held her head in her hands as if it might explode. It was scary. 'I've spent my whole loan for the rest of the term,' she said. 'I've got totally into debt. I won't be able to pay my college bills.'

'Is that all?' I was amazed. It was only money trouble. 'Why don't you just ask Mum and Dad to give you a bit more?'

Tamsin sighed, and poured the tea. 'The thing is,' she went on, 'I made a bargain with Mum and Dad before I left for uni not to get into debt. So to keep from getting overdrawn at the bank, I've been borrowing from my friends. But now they're getting hard up and they want their money back.'

'Harsh!' I sighed. 'But what can I do?' It seemed hopeless.

'Well,' said Tam, and she blushed deeply. Her face went almost puce. 'What I was thinking . . . well, it is a terrible cheek I know, but I was hoping . . . I was hoping you could do me a bit of a loan. How much have you got in your savings account?' she asked, urgently. I was startled.

'Uhhh, about £137,' I said hesitantly. 'You know, I'm saving up for our Newquay trip this summer. With Chloe and Toby and Fergus and everybody.'

'Well, that £137 would be fine, for a start,' said Tamsin, looking embarrassed and ashamed. 'I'm so sorry, Zoe. I'm so, so sorry . . .'

'It's all right,' I said, though I did feel majorly shocked.

'And then I was wondering if you could possibly have a whip-round among your friends,' Tam went on. 'I'd pay them back as soon as my next student loan cheque comes in. It's only a couple of months. And I'm going to get a job in the Easter hols, so I'll be able to pay everybody a bit back even earlier.'

I was stunned. Tamsin wanted me to go round collecting cash from my friends! How could I ever do that?

'You could pretend you were doing a sponsored thing for charity,' said Tamsin, looking faintly giddy and sick with guilt.

I was really shocked. I mean, I was sorry for Tamsin, but she had got herself into this jam by spending money on fab clothes and interior decor. You could hardly compare that with starving children in Africa. I didn't dare say anything, though, because she looked so depressed. She got up and walked to the window, looked out, and sighed.

'I hate myself,' she said. 'I've even thought of dealing drugs as a way of getting money.'

'Tamsin!' I shouted, leaping up. 'NEVER say anything like that again! Don't worry about a thing. It'll be easy-peasy. I know heaps of people with loads of money.' I didn't, of course. 'Toby and Fergus are saving up for Newquay too, and so's Chloe. Between us we probably have about £600.' I put my arm around Tamsin and smiled reassuringly.

At the thought of the £600 Tamsin began to look a bit more cheerful. We had an enormous hug. She squeezed me tight and tears ran down her cheeks.

'You're an angel, Zoe,' she said in a snuffly, sobbing kind of voice. 'I hate myself for asking you to do this. I'll pay everybody back ages and ages before your trip to Newquay.'

'Of course you will,' I beamed. 'No problem! Now *please* may I have some toast?'

20

MONDAY 11.38 A.M.

A new life beckons . . .

'Never mind toast!' said Tamsin. 'I'm taking you out for a pizza in the rooftop cafe, and then we'll do the new Orlando Bloom movie, OK?'

'Tamsin,' I said patiently, feeling very old, 'this is all going to cost, right? Why don't we just stay here and have some toast? Your room is heaps nicer than the rooftop cafe anyway. Last time we went there we were ignored by that waitress with the sneery lip, remember?'

'Oh.' Tamsin looked a bit sad. 'Yeah. Right.'

'It's a new era, OK?' I reckoned she needed a stiff pep talk if we were ever going to get her new life off the ground. And if I was ever going to get my money back. 'It's called poverty chic.' The ghost of a smile crossed Tamsin's face as she got four slices of bread.

'I have to take them down to the kitchenette,' she said. 'We're not allowed toasters in our rooms, remember?'

We went down to the kitchenette. It was window-less and hideous with notices everywhere. PLACE RUBBISH IN BINS DO NOT LEAVE ON FLOOR, said one notice. CLEAR UP AFTER YOURSELFS, said another. Some clever dick had corrected YOURSELFS to YOURSELVES.

'I hate that,' said Tamsin. 'The cleaner can't help having poor English. She's from Gdansk.' Tamsin wiped all the work surfaces energetically, even though we were only using the toaster. Then she swept the floor.

'Why don't you get a job as a cleaner?' I said. 'That would bring in a few quid. Plus tips.'

'Cleaners don't get tips,' said Tamsin. 'I might get a job as a waitress. They get tips. And I could develop a sneery lip.'

The toast popped up and we carried it back to her room. It smelt great. It was cosy to be having toast with Tamsin. But there was an atmosphere of crisis all the same. It wasn't like my previous visits to her at uni: festive and carefree. Her huge debt hung over us like a black cloud.

And beyond that, my anxiety about truanting rumbled and flashed quietly but ominously, like a thunderstorm getting closer.

We had peanut butter on the toast, and the last of the cheese. Then we drank two glasses of the designer water from her little student fridge.

'This is the last of the bottled water,' I said sternly. 'We who practise poverty chic drink only water from the tap.'

Tamsin pulled a face. 'The tap water round here is disgusting,' she said. 'You can taste the chlorine.'

'Dad says you should only start to worry if you *can't* taste the chlorine,' I reminded her. 'That's when the microbes strike. Anyway, you can get those water filter jugs.'

'I wonder how much they cost?' mused Tamsin.

We shared her last wizened apple. Part of it was brown.

'I'm getting a bit tired of poverty chic already,' said Tamsin.

'No!' I cried, alarmed. 'Bad girl, Tamsin!' Sometimes I talk to her as if she's a dog. 'Poverty chic is only just beginning. Stop focusing on the poverty. Concentrate on the chic.'

'I'm not quite sure where the chic bit comes in,' frowned Tamsin.

'We wear simple clothes in black or white or grey,' I said. 'Like in an old film with Greta Garbo. We wear no make-up.'

'*No* make-up!?' screeched Tamsin. I have counted her lipsticks, and there are over fifty.

'OK, we only wear make-up at the weekends,' I said. 'And we don't buy any more make-up until the last of the old make-up is finished.'

'We only shop at charity shops?' said Tamsin, trying to get into this thing.

'No!' I cried. 'You really don't get it, do you? We *don't* shop.'

'We don't shop?' Tamsin looked truly flabbergasted. It was as if somebody had told her that the sun will not rise tomorrow.

'There are other things,' I said.

'What?' Tamsin looked blank. 'What?'

'We walk and run,' I said sternly. 'We drink lots of water. We eat raw fruit and veg – and protein. We lose loads of weight, and start to look fabulous.'

Tamsin looked at me rather critically, with narrowed eyes. I was on tricky ground here.

'How much do you weigh at the moment, Zoe?'

she asked. 'If you don't mind my asking?'

'It's a secret,' I said. 'But by next month I'll be way thinner, thanks to poverty chic.'

'There's no need for you to go through all this poverty chic business,' said Tamsin. 'I'm the one with the massive financial probs.'

'Uh, sorry?' I said. 'I thought the idea was that I give you a loan – and get all my friends to as well?'

'Sorry, sorry,' said Tamsin. She looked sick with guilt.

'Right!' I said. 'Let's go for a walk, and every time we pass a guy, we give him marks for sex appeal. That costs nothing.'

'Great idea!' Tamsin jumped up and grabbed her coat.

It was a sparkly day. There was the faintest hint of spring in the air. She took my arm, and we walked through the streets of the old town, with their pretty spires and courtyards. Then we walked down to the river.

Tamsin asked me what was going on in my life, and I told her about our fruitless quest to find beaux to escort us to the Earthquake Ball next Saturday, and our disastrous interviews with Matthew and Scott. When I got to the bit about the outbreak of farting,

Tam laughed out loud. It was a lovely sound. I realised it was the first time she'd laughed since I'd arrived. Poor Tamsin! She'd really got herself into a miserable trap with this money thing. I was determined to rescue her.

I also told her how Oliver was hoping to work on our dad's farm, and how he'd rung me in the middle of the interview with Scott.

'Pants,' she said sympathetically. 'Why don't you ring him back?'

I kind of shuddered and cringed. 'Maybe,' I said. 'I feel kind of terrified. I will, though, I will . . . but not today. I've got enough to worry about already.'

'And how's Chloe?' she asked. I told her about Chloe's strange infatuation with Beast Hawkins. Tamsin frowned. Of course she knew Beast, because she'd been in upper sixth last year, when he'd been in lower sixth.

'Hmmm, watch out for him,' she said. 'He's really, like, dangerous, you know?'

'What do you mean, exactly?' I asked. 'What does he do?'

'Ohhhh – he's bad news, Zoe. He's a heart-breaker. A seducer of innocent maidens. He's got that fatal charm. You have to resist it.'

'I find him repellent,' I said. 'His hair is the wrong shade of dark brown. Plus he acts as if he owns everybody. But I am really worried about Chloe.'

We walked down by the river. A professorish type walked past us. He had a scruffy beard, terrible old medieval glasses and a bright red nose.

'Two,' I said as we passed him.

'Minus two, Zoe!' said Tamsin. 'You're such a soft touch! Two, indeed!'

So far nobody had scored over five. We took particular pleasure in marking down very handsome men.

A glorious fair-haired pin-up jogged past. He was tall and blue-eyed, with muscular shoulders and long, strong legs.

'Four,' said Tamsin. 'Frightful hairy legs like an aardvark.'

'Smelt like an aardvark, too,' I giggled. 'Plus you could tell he had a tummy button like a gigantic prune.'

Tamsin laughed. We strolled on. A tiny little old man tottered along. He must have been about 186 years old. His three hairs were plastered carefully across his bald head, and a glittering drip hung from the end of his nose.

'Now you're talking!' said Tamsin. 'What a babe-magnet! Nine and a half.'

'Oh, certainly,' I agreed. 'Shall we kidnap him and keep him as a kind of pet in your room?'

'We're not allowed pets,' said Tamsin. 'But there's nothing in the rules about not having a sex slave.'

Tamsin seemed to be feeling better. I didn't think there was any danger now of her throwing herself in the river.

'Right,' said Tamsin. 'We've walked so much my legs are completely hollow, so we're going to have a hot chocolate in the Cosy Dive. I totally insist. But don't worry, we'll use money which I would have spent on lipstick – in the bad old days.' I secretly wondered whose money we were going to use, and suspected it was, in some bizarre way, mine.

21

MONDAY 3.52 P.M.

Fatal distraction . . .

We spent ages in the Cosy Dive. We gave several men two out of ten for sex appeal, and then we changed the game.

'Instead of marks for sex appeal,' Tamsin suggested, 'we should try and identify which animal or bird is their familiar – like in the Philip Pullman books. We can do that with women too.'

We ordered two more hot chocolates from a waitress who was, in some secret essential way, in league with a hedgehog.

'You're a darling,' said Tamsin. 'You've made me feel a zillion times better. I've started to believe that I can really take control of my life.'

'OK, but listen up: these hot chocolates are £1.20

each. We've had four. That's uhhh . . . £4.80. A jar of instant hot choc is what – £2 or something? For that you can have ten hot chocs back in your room.'

'God! I take back what I said about you being a darling,' scowled Tamsin (but playfully). 'You are, in fact, a tedious, preachy old toad.'

A bespectacled lecturer-type man entered the cafe, accompanied by a tarty girl wearing a leopardskin jacket.

'The owl and the pussycat have entered the building,' I whispered. Just at that moment, my mobile rang. I jumped like somebody woken up suddenly from a wonderful dream.

The caller ID number flashed up. Oh no! Somebody was calling me from home! I had totally forgotten to ring between two and three to leave a message that I was staying with Chloe. It was now nearly four o'clock!

'Hi?' I said, trying to sound cool and normal, although my heart was hammering like mad.

'Hi, Zoe!' Phew! It was Dad. Though the potential for disaster was still huge, he was at least not Mum. 'Just wondered if you could get some sausages on the way home. Mum's got to stay in Birmingham tonight, so I thought we could have a secret orgy of saturated fat.' I looked at my watch. Back in the real world, I would indeed be on my way home from school.

'Listen, Dad,' I said. 'I was just about to ring you. I'm sorry, but I need to stay over at Chloe's tonight. We've just been told we've got to do a big assembly tomorrow, and we've got to spend all evening working on it.'

'Why don't you come over here?' Dad asked with infuriating cheerfulness. 'Chloe would probably love some bangers and mash, too.'

'No!' I said. 'Thanks, Dad, but she wouldn't. Chloe's a proper vegetarian now. She won't eat anything that has ever been alive.'

'Vegetables would have something to say about that,' said Dad with irritating playfulness. 'If they could speak.'

Oh, stop trying to be entertaining, Dad, I thought, *and just ring off.*

'What's the assembly about?' he asked with exasperating curiosity. I tried to think of something Dad would never ever be interested in.

'Politeness,' I said. God, it sounded dull. I had hit the jackpot here.

'Politeness!' exclaimed Dad with delight. 'What a

fabulous idea! It's almost disappearing from our society.'

Shut up, Dad, I thought in desperation.

'Do you remember when Mum came home from that trip to New York?' he went on. 'She said the most amazing thing was how polite everybody was, in the shops and cafes and stuff. Polite and yet not obsequious. Do you know what obsequious is?'

'Yes,' I lied.

'It's a really interesting subject,' mused Dad. 'Politeness ... uhhhh, it's about personal space. It's about respect. It's about democracy ... Would you like me to give you some help?'

'NO!' I yelled. 'I mean, no thanks, Dad. We really have to do this ourselves, yeah?'

'OK,' said Dad sadly. 'Looks like I have to get through a lonely evening on my own, I suppose.'

'Go for it,' I urged him. 'Get some beers in. Have a pizza delivered. Watch football for hours without your womenfolk complaining.'

'OK,' said Dad. He sounded as if he was getting into the idea. 'Fine. Yes. Hope you do a great assembly. See you tomorrow, then.'

'Yes!' I said firmly. 'Love you. Have fun! Bye!'

I rang off and did a huge PHEW sigh at Tamsin.

She grinned and did the thumbs-up.

'So we're in business, then?' she asked.

'Totally sorted. Mum's in Birmingham.'

'OK, I suggest we go back to my room, have a shower, get changed into fabulous outfits, go to the bar and play pool all evening with Ronnie and Art.'

Ronnie and Art are Tamsin's gay friends. Ronnie is short for Ronaldinho, like the footballer. He tells people his dad is a drugs baron but actually he just boringly works in a soap factory.

We went back to Tamsin's room, drank some more water, renewed our poverty-chic vows, and then dolled ourselves up for our cheap night out. We had vowed to drink only water all evening but Ron and Art took pity on us and bought Tamsin a beer and me a lemonade. I have this strange disability. I just hate the taste of alcohol. Any alcohol. I'm such a nerd.

Still, I was dressed like a film star in one of Tamsin's posh frocks. Luckily we have exactly the same size feet, so she'd lent me a wicked pair of scarlet high-heeled shoes. Nobody who'd seen me in my nerdy travelling outfit this morning would have recognised me as the hunchback in the baseball cap.

I kept losing at pool, but Ronnie and Art were completely charming. And when I told them about

Chloe and our project to find beaux to take us to the Earthquake Ball, Art said, 'We'd take you – wouldn't we, Ronnie?'

I was just thinking for a mad moment how cool it would be for Chloe and me to be escorted to the Earthquake Ball by a couple of weird Latin American homosexuals, when my mobile rang again. Oh hell! This time the ID flashing up was Mum's mobile!

My blood ran cold. I held the mobile at arms's length.

'It's Mum!' I cried. Tamsin looked alarmed. 'What shall I do?'

'Ignore it! Ignore it!' she said. 'No! Switch it off! No, ignore it!' I threw it on a nearby seat, where it thrashed away to itself for a few more seconds, and then was still.

'It's died,' said Tamsin. 'Switch it off, for God's sake, Zoe. It'll ruin our evening.'

I was so tempted. But I sort of knew I really had to keep it switched on, because if there was any problem back home about where exactly I was, I needed to know about it. After a minute or two I tiptoed up to my phone. There was a message on my voicemail. I checked it out.

'Zoe!' It was Mum. And oh, my God, she was in

Anxiety Overdrive. 'Zoe! Where are you! What's going on? Ring me, please, as soon as you get this message! We know you weren't at school today, and we know you're not at Chloe's! We want to know what the hell you think you're playing at!'

Hmmm. It seemed the poo was about to hit the ceiling.

22

MONDAY 8.33 P.M.

Disaster . . .

'My cover's totally blown!' I screeched. 'I'll have to ring her! What can I say? What can I say?'

'Don't mention me!' said Tamsin, going pale. 'Don't tell her you're here with me!'

'Well, where the hell can I say I am, then?' I wailed. 'They know I'm not at Chloe's – they know I wasn't at school.'

'Say you've been kidnapped by a cocaine gang,' suggested Ronnie.

'We could *really* kidnap you if it would be any help,' said Art. 'Hey! How rich is your dad? This could be a smart career move, Art!'

'Our dad is penniless,' said Tamsin crisply. 'It's our mum who's rich. Anyway, this isn't a joke, guys, so

187

unless you've got any sensible ideas, shut *up*!'

'I've got to ring her now,' I said. 'Or she'll be on the phone to the police. I can't lie any more.'

'Say you and Chloe are at somebody else's,' said Tamsin.

'Look, she knows I wasn't even at school. I've got to come up with something *like* the truth. I'll say I talked to you and you sounded low, so I got worried and decided to come up and see you.'

'Don't mention the money, though!' hissed Tamsin. 'It can't be money! It can't be! What else? What else?'

'It can't be an illness,' I said. 'You know they're both total hypochondriacs.'

'Heartbreak?' suggested Ronnie. 'Some guy dumped you?'

'Brilliant!' said Tamsin. 'Brilliant! Yessss! Heartbreak! I was crying!'

'Wailing!' I added. 'Down by the river! You were planning to throw yourself in!'

'He was a total bastard!' said Tamsin, role-playing like mad. 'His name was ... what was his name?' Tom, her most recent boyfriend, was evidently ancient history.

'Henry? Brad? Gladstone?'

'*Gladstone?* What kind of a name is that? OK, his name was Henry. He was a posh git.'

'He was a posh git rugby player.'

'He was a posh git rugy player with fabulous blue eyes and the body of Mr Universe, though,' said Tamsin anxiously. 'Or why would I have gone for him in the first place? I'm not a total loser.'

'She might think you're emotionally unstable if you can't even deal with being dumped without getting suicidal thoughts,' said Art.

'I don't care! I don't care!' cried Tamsin. 'As long as she doesn't know I'm in debt!'

I dialled Mum's number. My hands were shaking. She answered right away, before it even rang properly, and her *voice* was shaking. The whole world seemed to be shaking.

'Zoe! Where are you?'

'I'm with Tamsin,' I said. 'It's OK, I'm fine.'

'It is NOT OK!' screamed Mum. 'I've been beside myself with worry! Whatever possessed you?'

'I talked to Tamsin last night,' I said, my voice sounding brittle and thin, 'and she was really upset about this guy. She was walking down by the river, and I was afraid she might do something silly, so I thought I'd better come up and see her right away.'

'Why didn't you tell me?' demanded Mum.

'Tamsin didn't want to worry you,' I said lamely.

'Didn't want to worry me?' shrieked Mum. 'I've been eating the bedspread here! Let me speak to Tamsin!' I handed the phone over. Tamsin listened, cringing.

'No, Mum – really – I didn't know Zoe was going to come up . . .' Blaming me, then. Nice one. 'She just kind of appeared . . .' More listening and cringing. 'Of course, of course. I told her it was stupid.' I clenched my fists. I might just have to hit Tamsin as soon as Mum hung up. More listening. 'Oh he was just – you know, a bastard . . . Harry . . . A rugby player . . . I know. I know. I really really liked him, though . . . I know. I know.'

Eventually it seemed the hurricane of Mum's fury had blown itself out. Tamsin said goodbye to her and handed the phone back.

'Now, listen, Zoe,' said Mum. 'First of all, tell Chloe to ring her mother. Her parents are obviously frantic, too.' A gulf opened beneath me. Should I admit that Chloe was not with us? Or should I cover for her? If she was answering her mobe, I could ring her right away and get her to call her parents.

I didn't have to actually lie to Mum about Chloe

being with me, because Mum kind of swept on.

'I've told Tamsin to put you on the next train home,' said Mum. 'And I'll tell Dad to meet the train. You have got to be in school tomorrow, do you hear?'

'OK,' I said dismally.

'I want you to ring me from the landline when you've arrived back home, no matter how late it is.'

'All right, Mum,' I said. 'I'm sorry.'

'You'll be the death of me,' Mum said crisply, and rang off. It was quite a horrid way to say goodbye.

'I'll get the train times,' said Tamsin, picking up her mobile. I called Chloe. Thank God! She answered.

'Zoe? Whassup?'

'Listen!' I said. 'Our cover's blown. My mum knows I wasn't at school, and she knows I'm not at your house, and she thinks you're here with me and Tamsin, and she's ordered us to come home on the next train.'

'Zoe, you idiot!' yelled Chloe – with diabolical unfairness. 'How the hell am I going to sort this out?'

'Where are you anyway?' I said. 'With Beast Hawkins, I presume?'

'What if I am?' demanded Chloe angrily. 'OK, so I am with him. But it's not like you think. I'm just having a totally innocent night with him, for charity.'

'What?' I asked irritably. 'Snogging for Oxfam? Well, ring your mother. That's all I ask. Because if you don't, you're going to end up on the news tonight as a Missing Person.'

Chloe sighed and rang off, without saying goodbye. As if I'd got her into *her* mess as well as getting myself into *mine*.

And her mess was frankly, ludicrous. I was amazed at her stupidity. Spending the night with Beast Hawkins? On a weekday? For 'charity'? Who was she trying to kid? Where was all her famous intelligence and restraint? Up till now Chloe had been the most strait-laced, sensible girl in the class. Now she was behaving like some kind of demented slapper. Maybe Beast had plied her with horrid drugs! Maybe what was happening was date rape!

I shuddered with horror. Still, I couldn't sort out Chloe's problems. Trying to sort out Tamsin's had got me into one huge mess. I heaved a sigh, and took off the red high heels. They were suddenly starting to hurt.

'Better go back to your room and change,' I said sadly.

'There's a train at 9.25 p.m.,' said Tamsin. 'You'll

be back there by 10.30 p.m. I'd better ring Dad.'

As we walked back to her room, she called Dad and told him what time I would arrive. Then apparently he asked to speak to me.

'Sorry, Dad,' I said guiltily. 'I didn't mean to worry you.'

'Promise you'll never do anything like that again,' said Dad. 'I have torn out most of my remaining hair.' He sounded so much more relaxed and friendly than Mum, though. 'Promise you'll never lie to me, as well,' he said. 'All that stuff about the Politeness Assembly was total fiction, too, wasn't it?'

'Oh no,' I assured him hastily. 'That was all true.' I so *had* to arrange to do an assembly on politeness, as soon as possible, just to make Dad happy and prove to him I hadn't been lying about that bit.

'And what was all that about my farm?' said Dad. My brain reeled sideways.

'What?' I asked. 'Your f-farm?'

'That's how we knew you weren't at school today,' said Dad. 'Some guy rang up and asked if he could work on my farm. What was his name? Oliver?'

'Oliver Wyatt,' I said with a sickening, collapsing feeling spreading through my entire tum.

'That's right, Oliver,' said Dad. 'He said he'd

wanted to fix up some work for the hols, and because you weren't at school today, he'd decided to give us a call.'

Oliver Wyatt! Oliver Wyatt had actually phoned while I was away! And spoken to Dad about his 'farm'!

'What did you say?' I asked, sinking into deepest misery.

'Well, I told him I didn't have a farm, of course, you idiot,' said Dad. 'We're not all hooked on lying, you know.'

Oliver Wyatt knew I'd lied to him about Dad having a farm. He must now think of me as the most pathetic, lame, nerdy idiot in the entire school. And from tomorrow at 9 a.m. I would be in constant danger of bumping into him round a corner, and hearing his diabolical, mocking laugh. Oh, and I had to borrow £800 off my friends to stop my sister being arrested for debt. Apart from that, life was just dandy.

23

TUESDAY 8.48 A.M.

Horrid money moments . . .

Next morning, I reported to Mr Powell and was given a severe talking to. I told him about Tamsin's crisis. Not the real financial crisis – the fictional heartbreak crisis. It made no difference. I was on a warning, and all my teachers had to sign me in and out of lessons for a month.

I had missed registration because of my session with Mr Powell, and after that it was double art. Chloe doesn't do art. She opted for business studies, so we didn't meet until break. I found her by the tuck shop. She looked very pale. She grabbed me.

'Zoe!' That was all she said. She looked almost as if she might be going to cry.

'Chloe!' I said. 'What was going on last night? Did

you get home OK?'

'I rang my mum,' she said. 'And she said it was all right to stay where I was.'

'*Whaaaaaat?*' I gasped. I know Chloe's mum is a lot more liberal than mine, in an old hippy sort of way, but this seemed a bit extreme. 'They let you *stay the night* at Beast's?'

'I wasn't at Beast's,' said Chloe, looking jittery. 'We were at an Amnesty vigil in the high street. You know, like, uh – kind of demonstrating on behalf of political prisoners. And collecting money for their campaign. We were in a sort of cage thing like a prison.'

'What? All night?' I was amazed. 'Were you sitting on the actual pavement? Wasn't it freezing? Was there a loo? Did you have to pee in public?'

'There was a loo just around the corner,' said Chloe. 'At a petrol station. They let us use it. And we had mattresses. And blankets. And candles.' It sounded almost romantic.

'So was this just you and Beast?' I enquired. 'Or did you have a chaperone?'

'It was me and Beast and Gareth and Jennie,' said Chloe. I felt instantly rather jealous of these new friends. But I needn't have. I could see Chloe's chin begin to tremble. 'I've been really stupid, Zoe,' she said in a quavery voice. 'I really thought Beast was, you know, like, interested in me. After he said all those things and kissed me in the back of Donut's car. But it was like *totally obvious* that he fancied this Jennie girl. He was hitting on her right in front of me!'

'Never mind,' I said. 'Just try and forget all about him, OK?'

'It was horrendous,' said Chloe. 'I feel just, well – humiliated. He just amuses himself by flirting with me if there's nobody more attractive around. He must think I'm a total loser.' She was shaking now. Always a bad sign.

'Who cares what he thinks?' I tried to cheer her up. 'Ignore him. Move on. At least you did a brilliant thing for the political prisoners. I'll support you. You can have my last fiver.' I fished it out of my pocket. A thin but grateful smile crept across Chloe's face.

'Oh, Zoe, thanks so much!' she said in a trembly voice. I put my arms around her. 'You are so fantastic!'

'I've got just a little tiny favour to ask in return,' I said, holding her close because I couldn't say this face to face. 'Could you possibly lend me some money?

Just lend? Not for very long? Just till Easter – or at the very latest, a couple of weeks after Easter?'

Chloe escaped from my hug and looked a bit thoughtful.

'OK, it's possible,' she said. 'How much do you need?'

'Oh, just, well . . .' I said, trying to make it sound very little, 'uhhhh, how much could you manage? I mean, what's in your Newquay fund? £200?'

At this point Chloe fainted. I think it was mainly the lack of sleep, to be fair. Somebody called a teacher, and I put her in the recovery position even though, as she was wearing a short skirt, it meant you could see her knickers.

They were quite nice knickers actually, with butterflies on. I made a mental note to ask her where she got them.

Miss Donaldson came and Chloe, by now recovering, was helped off to the medical room. As the bell had gone, Miss D told me to go to my next lesson. Toby and I went to the medical room at lunchtime and discovered Chloe had been sent home. Her mother had come to fetch her, I expect, in her weird old hippie camper van covered with Greenpeace stencils.

'So,' I said. 'She's spent a night with Beast, but it was all in aid of Amnesty.'

'If I ever get to spend a night with anybody,' said Toby, 'it'll be in aid of myself, darling!'

'Listen, Tobe,' I said, taking his arm, and strolling with him towards the school field. 'I have a problem.'

'Houston, we have a problem,' said Toby. 'We've lost the lipstick!'

I laughed, but I hoped he was going to take this seriously. I had to get some support from somewhere. Chloe had gone into a coma rather than lend me money. Toby wasn't going to escape so easily.

I told him about my trip to see Tamsin, and her financial problems, and I laid it on really thick. Toby listened carefully.

'So basically, Tobe, I'm looking for loans,' I said. 'Big loans, but short-term.'

'Oh,' said Toby, looking vaguely shocked. 'Right.'

'Listen, Tobe,' I switched to my serious voice. 'How much have you got saved up for Newquay?' Toby hesitated.

'£280.56,' he said.

'Lend it me!' I begged. Toby's eyebrows flared. 'It's just to pay Tamsin's college bill. Then she's getting a job in the Easter hols, and she'll earn enough to pay most of it back right away.'

Toby thought for a moment, then offered me his hand. 'Done!' he said. I blinked. I could hardly believe it. We shook hands, then I flung my arms around his neck.

'Toby, you are an angel!' I gasped. I was so, *so* thrilled. I shut my eyes tight and gave him an extra-hard squeeze. Toby did a squeaky wheeze, like a very old teddy bear.

I laughed, opened my eyes, and looked over Toby's shoulder. And what did I see? Strolling towards us across the grass, and accompanied by a sixth-form girl with particularly long slim legs, was Oliver Wyatt! Hell's Bells and Buckets of Spit! Toby couldn't save me from *this* one.

24

TUESDAY 1.04 P.M.

Blanked and gutted . . .

For a moment I didn't know whether to go on hugging Toby or to fall hastily out of his arms. The moment Oliver Wyatt appears, everything is so damned complicated. If he hadn't recognised me yet, he might not recognise me *at all* if I stayed wrapped around Toby, hiding my face in his chubby old neck. On the other hand, if Oliver had recognised me, I didn't want him to think I wanted to be wrapped around Toby, like *ever*.

Although God knows I was never going to be even remotely wrapped around Oliver. All I wanted, at this moment, was to be in Australia. I fell briskly backwards out of Toby's embrace and hit him playfully across the chops, just to prove to anybody in the area that the hug had been meaningless. They could see I would just as soon beat him up, in an affectionate way, of course, as one might beat up a brother.

Toby looked a bit surprised, and started to say something. I hadn't the faintest idea what he was saying. My head was full of loud noise. Later I realised it must have been the blood pounding round my brain. But right then all my previous history with Oliver Wyatt kind of flashed before my eyes – like, at the moment of death, when we apparently get a high-speed replay of our whole lives.

I first really got into Oliver a year ago, in a school play. He was dressed in black playing some sombre knight in a medieval epic. He didn't say much, but he looked so handsome, my bra straps kind of burned into my shoulders with excitement. Then a couple of weeks later, I'd been sitting on the upper deck of a bus, and I'd been relaxing and looking down at the street, and suddenly there he was – going into a bookshop!

My heart literally exploded all over the roof of my mouth. Instantly I jumped up, raced down the bus stairs, got off at the next stop, and hurtled at 100 mph back to the bookshop, where I failed to find any trace of him *whatever.* But it was proof I was hooked, and the fact that Oliver had recently been in the bookshop gave it a fabulous glamour.

And Oliver was approaching! Right now, in the real world! I could see him coming up behind Toby. Although, of course, I wasn't actually looking at Oliver, but desperately avoiding eye contact. However, somehow, although I wasn't looking at him at all, I could see nothing else.

I prepared myself in anguish for the mocking jests I knew he would toss in my direction, about my delusions on the farm front and preposterous lies involving piglets. At the same time, my brain was still treating me to a hectic flood of memories: Oliver glimpsed by the geography room, by the boys' loos, by the school office, by the Dolphin Cafe . . .

He was now so close to us that I could feel my skeleton melting. I cringed, waiting for Oliver's cruel aside. Toby was still rabbiting on about something, thank God. Bless him! Technically I was having an out-of-body experience and dear old Tobe didn't have an inkling.

Oliver Wyatt loomed, on my left, and passed me. The air which had blown playfully across his skin entered my nostrils. My nose hairs secretly burst into flame. But he said nothing. He even slightly turned away from me, as his companion, the sixth-form girl with the endless legs, was on the other side of him, and laughing.

Seconds later, I assume, though to me it seemed like centuries, he had passed me and gone. And there had been no cruel jests. The total swine! He had blanked me! He would never speak to me again! I was beneath contempt! Worthless! Not even deserving of a cruel jest or mocking laugh! No piss taken.

Possibly he was so enchanted with his leggy companion that he didn't want her to know that I had ever spoken to him, let alone lured him with my tales of fabulous piglets. I was totally gutted at this evidence that I was nothing to him – perhaps even less than nothing.

What a wasted opportunity! I had actually spoken to the legend that is Oliver Wyatt, in the hospital when I was with Donut – *spoken* to him, and blown it. He'd given me his card, dammit! It had been my chance to appear confident, charismatic and attractive, and instead I had come across as a lying, shrieking chav and a slapper – literally – of defenceless young men.

'Would that be OK?' said Toby, finishing his sermon.

'Would what be OK?' I asked, blinking. 'I'm so sorry, Toby, I just switched off there for a moment and had a total brainstorm. Carry on.'

'Well, I just said I could get the money for you today after school,' said Toby, 'if you like. And you could get it to your sister tomorrow or whatever.'

'Toby, you are a babe!' I cried, flinging my arms around him once again. He kind of flinched. 'I shall never be able to repay you – I mean, in the ultimate sense! Not in the financial money-type sense – of course I'll be able to repay you that, but this is such a big deal! You are a darling!'

Just then Fergus turned up, and Toby told him all about Tamsin's problems and how we were all going to rally round and empty our piggy banks. Fergus looked a bit uneasy.

'I'mNotSure,' he gibbered. 'IDunno . . . LeaveIt WithMeOK?'

'Tight git,' Toby whispered to me later. 'Don't worry, I'll get it out of him.'

I was deeply deeply grateful to Toby for being the best friend in the world. But in a way it all seemed to be taking place far away and even long ago. The real me was trapped in some kind of hysterical bubble in cyberspace with only this fact: Oliver Wyatt hated me so much, he couldn't even be bothered to take the piss.

That night I called by at Chloe's. Her mum, Fran, opened the door. Her thick grey hair was down to her shoulders this time, which in my view is a style disaster. Mum's hair is always nicely cut and tinted. Chloe's mum's hair is hardly ever even brushed.

'Oh, hello, Zoe,' said Fran. 'Come in. Chloe's up now. She had a huge sleep. I think she was just over-tired from her Amnesty vigil.'

Chloe was lying on the sofa, wearing PJs and watching TV. Her mum went back to her funny little old fortune-teller's table in the corner and started messing about with some books and papers. She's not a professional fortune-teller. She just reads the tarot for fun. The table is round and covered with a sort of carpet, and behind it on the wall is a sort of purple tapestry curtain thing, so it's all a bit picturesque.

'Let's go upstairs,' said Chloe, switching off the TV. 'Don't want to disturb Mum – she's writing a poem about stars.' She gave me a meaningful wink. Clearly privacy was our first priority.

We trudged up to Chloe's little room, which is always cosy and tidy but kind of drab. If only she was more into colour. She's also got a horrible kind of tank thing in the corner where she used to keep her pet toads and poison frogs and things. (All now, thank God, gone to froggy heaven.) I sometimes think her previous love of slimy creatures has shaped her taste in boys. We sat on her bed.

'My life is in ruins,' said Chloe.

'So's mine,' I replied.

'OK,' said Chloe. 'Who's going to go first?'

'Let's toss for it,' I said, getting a coin out of my purse. I flicked it up towards the ceiling. It glittered in the lamplight, somehow reminding me of how much money I had to try and get my hands on for Tamsin.

'Tails,' said Chloe. This struck me as odd, as she usually says '*heads*'. And tails it was.

25

TUESDAY 7.32 P.M.

Not completely convincing . . .

'OK,' said Chloe, 'I've been totally stupid. Beast just used me. It's so humiliating! He just snogged me for fun. Kind of because I was there. I mean, if you'd been in the back of that car with him, he'd have snogged you.'

I wanted just to sympathise with Chloe, but what she'd said sounded faintly insulting somehow – as if it meant, *Beast would have snogged anybody, even you.* I knew she didn't really mean it like that. But there was something else about it that I didn't like.

'I wouldn't have *let* him snog me,' I said. Instantly I regretted it. It made me seem kind of toffee-nosed and superior. I hadn't meant it to.

'Huh!' said Chloe. 'I'd like to see you try to stand

up to him!'

'No, no,' I said, 'the thing is, I don't fancy him, Chloe. And you do, don't you?'

Chloe blushed. 'I *did*,' she admitted. 'But now I hate him.'

'Good. Because at one point I was beginning to think he'd ask you to go to the Earthquake Ball with him.'

Chloe blushed again. 'I would never even *consider* going to the Earthquake Ball with him, even if he wasn't going with Lauren Piper.'

The way she said '*Lauren Piper*' tried to sound free and easy, as if Lauren was a major buddy, but I suspected that secretly Chloe was longing to transform Lauren into salami. As for all that '*I hate Beast*' rubbish, only last Sunday – a mere two days ago, though it seemed more like two years – she'd said, '*Beast is really just a pussycat. He's absolutely adorable. He's not at all like people say. He said I was beautiful.*' She said she hated him, but could I trust her to stick to her hate?

'Never mind him,' said Chloe, sticking out her lower lip. Then she gave me a kind of anxious, guilty look.

'I'm really really sorry about the babysitting,' she said. 'I know I majorly let you down. I'm *so* sorry,

Zoe. If only I'd gone babysitting with you instead of letting Beast take me to that horrible Next Big Thing! It was awful, Beast and Donut coming round to the Normans' house and waking up the twins and stuff. It was all my fault. Were the parents really cross? Did they give you a hard time?'

'It's kind of a big muddle,' I said. 'She was cross, so then I said I'd better not babysit for them any more, then she chased me down the street and begged me to reconsider.'

'So will you never have to go there again?' asked Chloe, looking mightily relieved.

'I don't know,' I sighed. 'It was all left up in the air. They didn't pay me, either. I kind of left in a huff, sort of.'

'Oh God!' Chloe cringed. 'I'm so sorry, Zoe. That was all my fault. I should have come babysitting with you. I was really mean. I hate myself.'

'No need for melodrama,' I assured her, biting my thumbnail (which I'd suddenly noticed was ragged). 'Just never let it happen again, you bitch.'

'Never!' promised Chloe. 'You're my best mate, and if I ever let you down again may I be nibbled to death by poison toads.' She stared solemnly at me and drew her finger across her own throat. Then she reached for her notebook and clicked her pen in a businesslike way. 'OK,' she said. 'Let's get back to the Ball. Let's draw up another shortlist of boys who seemed too nerdy to consider last week. They might have matured unexpectedly in the last few days.'

'Wait!' I said. 'You haven't heard about how *my* life is in ruins, yet. Some best mate you are!'

'Oh?' said Chloe. 'Is there more? Sorry. Tell me all about it. If anybody's giving you a hard time, I'm going to eat them alive.'

'Oh yeah?!' I raised an eyebrow quizzically. 'Forgive me, but don't you only eat beans on toast?'

I told her all about my awful bungled attempt to get to know Oliver, and his blanking me on the school field. She made a few sympathetic sounds, but to be honest she looked as if, somewhere in her heart of hearts, she was thinking about something or somebody else.

Then I told her all about Tamsin's probs. This time Chloe did seem sympathetic. She adores Tamsin. I think it's partly because whenever they meet, Tam always says, 'Oh, Chloe! You look absolutely *fabulous*!' even if Chloe's wearing a tired old sack with maggots literally peeping out of the ragged edges.

'Poor Tam! I'll lend you all the money I can lay my hands on,' said Chloe, going to her special drawer and taking out a cash box. She unlocked it with a dainty key and took out a huge wad of notes.

'Here you are,' she said. 'Let's count it. It's my Newquay money, plus a bit my grandpa gave me for my birthday last month . . . uhhh, £225.' And she just handed it over.

I was startled. It seemed too easy. Chloe's generosity just took my breath away. I was also just a teeny tad worried about the amount of money Chloe and Toby had already managed to save up for Newquay. I hadn't really got cracking with that, yet. I made a mental note to get a job in the Easter holidays.

'I'll get you an envelope,' said Chloe. She went downstairs. I just sat staring at the big wodge of money. I don't think I'd ever held that much in my hand before. Chloe's mum doesn't believe in banks. She says they're all crooks. So their house is full of little stashes of money. I hope they're never burgled. It is unlikely, because Geraint would eat burglars alive, head first, without even waiting to be introduced.

Chloe returned with an envelope. She put the

money in it and handed it back to me. I felt, frankly, nervous.

'I'll give you a receipt or something . . .' I hesitated. 'An IOU . . .'

'Oh, no, don't bother with that, Zoe,' said Chloe, sitting down again and getting out her notebook. 'I know you'll pay me back. I have complete faith in you, you idiot!' And she grinned in a breezy way which was, of course, adorable, but somehow made me feel rather nervous, deep down.

OK, she could trust *me*, but what about Tamsin? Would Tam come up with the goods? Would she really get a job at Easter? Was she still living the virtuous life of poverty chic even though I wasn't actually there to forbid her the designer water and the charity-shop pearls?

'I'll just call Tam, now,' I said suddenly. 'And tell her how brilliant everybody's been.'

'OK,' said Chloe, doodling in the margin of her notebook. She seemed to be drawing a face. A male profile. With long dark hair and magnetic eyes. Hmmm. A pirate, perhaps? I was a bit worried about Chloe. There have been times when she hasn't been completely honest with me. Usually it's been when her pride is involved. I had a feeling this could be one of those times.

'Hi, Zoe!' Tamsin answered. She sounded much better: happy and upbeat. I could tell she was in the college bar. There was music in the background and people yelling all around her. 'How's everything?'

'It's going brilliantly!' I told her. 'Toby and Chloe have lent me loads of money. I've got nearly £650 already. Fergus probably won't be able to, but I'm sure we can get enough to pay your friends back.'

'Well done, Zoe!' shrieked Tam. 'You are an AAAAAAngel!' She sounded a bit drunk, to be honest.

'Tamsin,' I said, trying to sound light-hearted because I didn't want Chloe to get worried about her loan, 'you're still on the straight and narrow, aren't you? Still doing poverty chic?'

'God, yes!' shouted Tam. 'I'm so poor, they've told the Pope! I eat out of rubbish bins! I wear only rags! OK, I've had a couple of gin and tonics tonight, but Ronnie treated me! I sleep on bare boards, the lot. Don't worry, darling. I am totally *but tot*ally on board. And I'm going to sell all my throws and stuff on eBay, just like you suggested.'

'And your clothes?' I asked. I didn't want to nag, but . . . 'or some of your clothes, anyway?'

'Yeah, yeah!' gabbled Tam. 'All of my clothes!' She laughed in a mad, off-the-wall kind of way. 'All my clothes, babe! I'm going to do poverty chic in the complete and utter nude!' She squealed with laughter. I hesitated. I didn't want to nag. And I didn't want to say anything that would make Chloe lose faith in Tam and perhaps start regretting handing me her entire worldly wealth in an envelope.

But I so wanted to say something, something boring maybe, something preachy maybe. Just something about what a big deal it was for my friends to give her all their money like this, and how mega-important it was for her to take it seriously, and not mess about as if it was some gigantic joke.

It didn't seem quite the right time or place, however. So I kept my mouth shut, and after a few more jokes and expressions of undying sisterly affection, we said goodbye.

'OK,' said Chloe. 'Let's be totally rational about this Earthquake Ball thing. What boys do we know who would be, well, tolerable?' We tried to think of tolerable boys. There were none.

Suddenly the baby laughed in my handbag. I snatched up my phone. I didn't recognise the caller ID.

'Hello?' said a deep thrilling masculine voice.

'Oliver?' I cried, leaping up in my ecstasy and almost starting to dance.

'No – it's Matt.'

'Matt?' I pulled a face at Chloe and shrugged. Who the hell was Matt?

'Matthew,' said the voice. 'Matthew Kesterton. You interviewed me last Sunday about the life coach job.'

'Oh, Matthew!' I cried. 'Of course! I'm so sorry!' Terror seized my soul. I was going to have to tell him he hadn't got the job. 'I'm sorry I haven't got back to you . . . I've been out of town. My sister needed a bit of help . . .'

'It's OK,' said Matthew. It was amazing how warm and deep and lovely his voice was, when you couldn't see his strange robo-pastiness and his unsmiling khaki eyes.

'Look, Matthew, I'm sorry the interview didn't go very well . . .' I stammered. 'It was – we haven't actually chosen anybody yet . . .' I just couldn't face telling him he was not The One.

'No, that's fine,' said Matthew. 'I wasn't calling you to hassle you about that. I mean, I wouldn't want to put you under pressure. It's something else.'

'Oh?'

'No, uh, I was ringing you to ask . . .' Matthew hesitated, sounding not quite as confident as usual. For a second my blood ran cold. Was he going to ask me for a date? Had he been swept off his feet by my fabulous farting? 'I wanted to ask if I could have a session?' he asked.

'A – session?' It sounded a little bit strange, and to be honest, possibly sleazy.

'A life coaching session,' said Matthew. 'I think I could learn a lot from it. How much do you charge? Thirty-five an hour? That's the normal rate, I believe?'

'Oh – uh – yes,' I stuttered, totally gobsmacked.

'That's fine,' said Matthew. 'So when could you fit me in? It would have to be after 4.30. Would that be possible?'

'Oh yes,' I said faintly. 'Sure. How about tomorrow?'

'Would five o'clock be OK?' suggested Matthew.

'Fine,' I replied, desperate to escape from this disastrous appointment but unable to make the right move.

'Same place?' asked Matthew.

'Yes,' I croaked. My mouth had gone dry with

embarrassment. At this moment I remembered I should have been using my squeaky voice. But it seemed the least of my problems, to be honest.

'OK, then,' said Matthew. 'See you then. Bye!' And he rang off.

'What on earth was that all about?' asked Chloe. I told her. She went pale. 'What do life coaches do, exactly?' she pondered.

'Let's get online,' I commanded, 'and find out.'

26

WEDNESDAY 4.03 P.M.

Poised to pounce on our prey . . .

Next day, at school, life was one long pretence. I pretended to have done my homework. Then I had to pretend that Tam was going to pay everybody back soon. I pretended that I didn't care if Oliver came round the corner at any minute. (He didn't, thank God.) And now school was over I had to pretend to be a life coach.

This was the worst bit, really. Interviewing Matthew had been such a disaster that the thought of seeing him again made me feel slightly sick. However, for some reason I'd agreed to it, so here we were. On the way home we stopped in the charity shop and I picked over a few men's shirts. I selected three: brown, taupe and a kind of soft gold.

'What about blue?' asked Chloe, holding up a terrible T-shirt with dolphins on it.

'Leave the colours to me,' I said with a sigh. I sometimes think Chloe is sort of colour-blind. 'Trust me. Stick to what you're good at.'

'What's that?' asked Chloe, panicking.

'Panicking,' I told her.

The shirts cost practically nothing. It was the one aspect of the life coach thing I was almost looking forward to. I was going to redesign Matthew's wardrobe. It might be fun. A bit like picking up where I had left off with my Barbie dolls all those years ago.

'How are we going to *do* this?' asked Chloe, panicking as we walked up her front path. 'Where do we *start*?'

We hadn't got very far with the Internet research into life coaching the night before. Most of the websites had been about how hard you had to train to be a life coach, with pictures of people standing on the tops of mountains looking fulfilled in a crazy kind of way and waving their arms about.

'What if he asks to see our certificates?' fretted Chloe. 'Do we say we've lost them or what?'

'If he asks to see our certificates,' I told her grimly,

'we might as well admit the whole thing was a con.'

'Oh no!' said Chloe, covering her mouth with her hand. It wasn't much to hide behind, but it was a start. 'You're going to have to run this, Zoe,' she went on, as we entered the house, 'because it's just totally, like, beyond me.'

Luckily Chloe's mum was out, so we had the place to ourselves. Swiftly we changed out of our school uniform into our cool life coach outfits. I barely had time to straighten my eyebrows and slap a bit of cover-up foundation on Nigel. Moments later the front doorbell gave its irritating buzz.

'Answer it! Answer it!' hissed Chloe, cringing back into her bedroom. She's such a wuss. Sighing, I went downstairs and opened the door.

'Hi!' said Matthew. He was wearing his suit again, and his hair was more ferociously slicked back than ever. I endured the cold, limp handshake and asked him in. Chloe came downstairs and greeted him with a nervous grin, but he didn't manage anything in the smile department in return – not even a friendly twitch of the lip.

'OK, Matthew!' I decided to jump in at the deep end. 'Let's get on with it. First impressions. What do you think is most important?'

'Ummm ... to be smartly dressed?' asked Matthew, pulling down the hem of his jacket in a self-conscious way.

'Hmmm – have to say no, not really!' I grinned. 'Try again?'

Matthew pondered deeply. 'To turn up on time?'

'Uhh, yes, that's important, but it's not what I'm driving at. OK, I'm now going to come into the room and greet you, twice. In two different ways.'

'What are you doing that for?' asked Chloe.

'You'll see.' I gave her a secret stare. She shouldn't question my methods. She shouldn't act as if this was all new to her. She was *hopeless*. I went out, then came into the room again with a totally serious straight face. 'Hello, Matthew.' I said, unsmilingly.

I approached him. He cringed slightly. 'How do you do?' I said, and extended a limp hand to him. He shook it, looking wary.

'OK!' I said, clapping my hands and trying to create a festive atmosphere, though both Matthew and Chloe looked deeply mystified and under-whelmed. 'Now I'm going to do that again!'

I went out and then came in again, beaming in a friendly way. 'Hello, Matthew!' I said, all cheery and sparkly. I then gave him a warm, firm handshake.

'OK,' I said. 'Which of those greetings did you prefer?'

Matthew thought for a minute. 'The first one?' he said. 'Because it was more, uh – businesslike?'

Oh God. I was going to have to go back to square one with him and help him to understand the concept of being human.

'Right, Matthew,' I said. 'Come over to the mirror with me.' There's a mirror in the corner by Chloe's mum's tarot table, where she once tried to contact the spirits of dead people by candlelight. But instead she only saw a few smears because Chloe hadn't cleaned the glass properly.

I positioned Matthew in front of the mirror. He looked sombre. In fact, this was as near as the mirror had ever come to reflecting a dead person. We stood side by side. In the background we could see Chloe slightly giggling. God, she was annoying sometimes.

'OK,' I said. 'Now think of the person in the world you are most fond of.'

Matthew looked very serious indeed.

'Uhhh,' he murmured, 'do you mean, people in my actual family, or people, like, in the media or films or whatever?'

'Oh, for God's sake, Matthew!' I shouted. 'I'm just

trying to get you to smile!' Matthew looked surprised.

'To smile?' he repeated, as if the concept was entirely new.

'A smile,' I said, 'is the first weapon in your attack.' Matthew looked a bit reassured that the smile might be considered as a weapon.

'Go on,' I said, grinning away merrily at him in the mirror, 'think of somebody funny. Think of Vicky Pollard. Or whoever makes you laugh on TV.'

Matthew looked at me in the mirror and smiled in a stiff, mad way. It was an obedient smile without any feeling whatever. I began to feel he might be better off just not trying to smile at all.

'Jolly good!' I assured him, lying through my teeth. My own smile now became stiff and mad also. Although by now his smile had vanished. In the mirror we could see Chloe laughing helplessly behind us.

'God!' I exclaimed, 'I don't know which is worse – trying to get you to laugh, or trying to get Chloe to stop laughing.' Suddenly, Matthew smiled. Properly! 'You smiled then!' I yelled. 'Bingo!'

Suddenly Chloe's phone rang. For an instant the samba chicken ringtone blotted out all civilised conversation.

'Hello?' she said, heading for the door. 'Oh, it's

you, is it? Listen – if I'd known it was you – whose phone? Well, that's just sneaky! . . . no, no, no!' She went out into the hall. She ran upstairs. It was obvious Beast had rung again.

'Matthew,' I said, 'your smile transforms your face. Look.' He looked into the mirror and smiled a genuine smile. He was thousands of miles away from having a fragment of Brad Pitt's charisma, but at least he looked alive.

'Now let's work on your handshake,' I said. Upstairs, we heard Chloe's bedroom door slam. 'OK, let's shake,' I said, holding out my hand. It was weird to be sort of almost holding hands alone. But I owed it to Matthew to get him to stop flopping his hand about like a dead fish and start cultivating a masculine squeeze.

'Squeeze my hand tighter!' I urged him. In the room above, Chloe started yelling. We couldn't hear the actual words, but it was obvious from her tone of voice that she was having a Grade-A phone row.

'Blonketing varly prangester forgest thumpwork!' she yelled.

'Ow!' I yelped as Matthew tightened his grip. 'Steady on, Matthew! I almost felt my bones splinter!'

'Effargst plinkworthy uf crapola mangking

wannabeef frickerstowe!' shouted Chloe, above.

Matthew loosened his grip slightly. He frowned with the tremendous challenge of shaking my hand with a kind of nice normal pressure.

'Imagine my hand is a can of Coke which you've just opened, and you're standing up in a bus, and you don't want to spill any,' I suggested. 'That's about the amount of pressure you need. You're not trying to crush the can for recycling, OK?' Phew! This life coach business was certainly a challenge. 'Right, Matthew, now go out of the room and come in and greet me,' I suggested. 'Gimme the teeth, the squeeze, the whole personality.'

Matthew went out, knocked, and came in with something like a smile on his face. He got his hand out far too early – in fact, his hand came round the door first, but he managed to shake hands without either disgusting me or cutting off my circulation. This was progress.

'Well done, Matthew!' I beamed. Matthew beamed back. He really did look almost quite nice, for a minute.

'Fargurn apsootoh crinkum parly avocettage oosha furgently barroooophicuss!' raged Chloe, up in her bedroom.

'Right,' I said, serenely ignoring the rumpus on the first floor. 'Come back over to the mirror, Matthew. We're going to do a little colour experiment with you.' I got out my charity-shop shirts.

'Strile pod nurst!' yelled Chloe.

We gazed into the mirror together. I held the brown shirt loosely in front of Matthew, covering up his boring grey suit and strange, upsetting purple tie.

'You should be thinking, *brown*,' I purred in his ear. 'Blonds – I mean fair guys – should always consider brown. Brown is the new black. It's ultra-chic. And it does loads for you, Matt. It brings out the topazy tones in your hazel eyes.'

'I nimmerwannarspiktyeraggin! Yra baaaathud!' shouted Chloe.

'Are my eyes really hazel?' asked Matthew. You could see he was on the verge of beginning to fancy himself.

'Yes,' I assured him. I was uneasily aware that Chloe was about to rejoin us. We heard her bedroom door slam. We heard her footsteps thundering downstairs. I think we both cringed slightly, to be honest.

'I always thought they were just brown,' said Matthew, looking back towards the door. We both watched Chloe come into the room. I was hugely, but *hugely* relieved that she wasn't crying. Not yet, anyway. She looked a bit flushed. Her eyes were bright. She had the look of a mad electric doll which had just been fitted with a brand-new battery.

'Matthew,' she said, in a deranged tone of voice, 'would you be interested in taking me to the Earthquake Ball next Saturday?'

27

WEDNESDAY 4.58 P.M.

I resort to the occult

Matthew turned to me and raised his eyebrows slightly. 'Is this part of the session?' he asked.

'No,' I said, heroically concealing my total fury at the way Chloe was acting, 'I think Chloe would really like you to escort her to the Ball. Is that right, Chloe?'

'Yes!' said Chloe. 'Please!'

'Er ... OK, thanks, fine ...' said Matthew, sounding massively uncertain about the whole thing. 'But ... uhhh ... I thought your name was Africa?'

'That's her professional name,' I said quickly. I felt as if I was acting in some dire reality TV series written and filmed in hell. 'Her real name's Chloe.'

Matthew looked impressed.

'Do you think I should have a professional name?' he asked me, in his laborious tortoise-like way. 'I've always sort of fancied Brad. I don't really think I am a Matthew, if you know what I mean? Do you? Do you think I'm more of a Brad?'

I managed, with a supreme effort, not to tell Matthew what I thought he was.

'No, no, Matthew!' I insisted. 'Matthew is heaps more stylish than Brad! Anyway – Brad, Africa, whatever – you two guys just sort out the details of your forthcoming trip to the Ball, while I fix us a drink!' I produced a really bitter, stinging grin and went out to the kitchen.

How could Chloe just lose it like that? Asking Matthew to take her to the Ball when we hadn't even discussed it? What if I wanted him to go with me? After all, I'd been the one doing all the door-opening and life-coaching and hand-shaking, dammit.

I'd lost track of the times her random impulses had cut across plans we'd both agreed on. I was absolutely fuming. My hands were shaking with rage. I put the kettle on. If ever I'd needed a cup of Chloe's mum's Serene Clouds Yogi Tranquillity Tea, that time was now.

I stared out of the kitchen window at Fran's bird-table. Frenzied blue tits were quarrelling over the nuts. How uncomplicated their lives were. I wished I was a bird. But I didn't feel like a sweet little garden bird. I felt like a huge ferocious eagle hovering above a crag, with bloodstained claws and a murderous beak.

A few moments later, Chloe came in. 'What do I do now?' she whispered. 'We've fixed up all the stuff about the Ball, but what's the next life coach thing he's got to do?'

I resisted the temptation to swoop down and tear her head off with my tremendous claws. I just flashed my eyes so fiercely they actually hurt, flared my nostrils so wide you could have driven a train up them, and let rip in a homicidal whisper. The kettle was coming to the boil with loads of steam and a menacing rumble. And so was I.

'Don't ask *me* what to do next!' I hissed. 'Since you always do just what you feel like anyway! I am sick – just totally *sick* of the way you ruin everything. You never listen! You never remember what we've agreed on for more than five seconds! You never show any consideration for what I might want! You're just a total freakin' nightmare!'

Chloe's eyes went absolutely huge. She was

silenced. In the silence, the kettle came to the boil and clicked. And there was a tap on the door.

'Come in!' I yelled, turning my back on Chloe and getting out a couple of mugs.

Matthew kind of edged his way around the door. In normal life I would have worried that he'd over-heard, but right now, frankly, I couldn't care less.

'Excuse me,' he said. 'Could I possibly use your toilet?'

'Not toilet, Matthew!' I snapped. 'Loo, OK? Show Matthew to the loo, Chloe!' My mum hates the word 'toilet' and I realised that, in my dreadful mood, I sounded just like her off on one of her snobby tirades.

Chloe went out and showed Matthew to the loo. I made two cups of coffee. I was still shaking with rage and my heart was pounding. After Chloe had showed Matthew to the downstairs cloakroom, I heard her go upstairs to the bathroom and lock herself in. What now? A storm of hygienic weeping? A massive sulk? Like I cared.

I carried the coffees into the sitting room and placed them on the coffee table. I didn't want any. I would never drink again. Or eat. I would just soar in the sky and plummet down and tear the heads off living things. Especially living things that looked a bit like Chloe. Not for food – just for fun.

Moments later Matthew returned. I'll say this for him, he was a swift urinator. It was a desirable attribute. He should put it on his CV, along with his typing speeds.

'So . . .' he said. 'What next? There's about . . .' he looked at his watch '. . . fifteen minutes left, yeah?' I didn't like that *yeah*. It belonged with *Brad*, the transatlantic identity he craved. 'Would you like me to come into the room a few more times?' he asked. 'Kind of, practise the Meet and Greet thing a bit?'

'No!' I cried, almost in a desperate shriek. I couldn't face the thought of having to talk to him *at all* about *anything*, even in the virtual reality of our earlier pointless session.

For an instant, my mind went blank. Then I noticed Chloe's mum's desk. I took a piece of paper from there, and placed it in front of him.

'Write a short essay,' I commanded. 'Just a few paragraphs. Call it *"My aims and aspirations, short-term, medium-term and long-term"*.'

'Could I have a book to rest on?' asked Matthew. I handed him one of Fran's movie stars photo books. It had Marilyn Monroe naked on the cover. I hoped it wouldn't distract him too much. Matthew turned it firmly over so Marilyn was invisibly sprawling all over his knees. He put the paper down, clicked his pen and started to write.

I was amazed at how he just did everything I asked without arguing. In some ways he would make a much better best mate than Chloe. When had she ever done something I suggested without arguing? All she ever did was lose it, blow it and ruin everything with her stupid impulsiveness.

I decided to have a cup of coffee after all. Chloe was probably going to sulk in the bathroom for at least the next half hour. I poured a little bit of milk in and was just stirring it quietly, trying to calm down, when the front door flew open and Geraint charged in and drove his snout in my face.

'Hi, Chloe, I'm home!' trilled Fran, in the hall. 'Can I smell coffee? *Larvely*!' She came into the sitting room. 'Oh, Zoe!' cried Fran. 'How *larvely!* Geraint, stop it! Can you stay to supper?' Then she clocked Matthew. 'Oh, hello!' she beamed.

Matthew put his essay to one side, stood up and shook hands with her. I could see him trying to exert the right kind of pressure. He produced a strange synthetic bloodcurdling smile. It kind of didn't fit him. It was three sizes too big for his face.

'This is Matthew,' I said. 'This is Chloe's mum. Matthew's just writing a short essay. We're working on a project.'

'An essay?' Fran sounded intrigued. 'What – is he doing your homework or something? You're not paying somebody to do your schoolwork, are you, Zoe?' Fran laughed raucously. I could tell she was half-enchanted by my business skills.

'No, no!' I smiled. 'I'm Matthew's life coach! Chloe just asked him to the Ball – so that's her partner sorted.'

'Really?' said Fran. 'Where is Chloe?'

'In the bathroom.' I tried not to sound too grim.

'I must just go and change out of this top,' said Fran. 'It's as hot as Hades.'

She ran upstairs. I heard her call to Chloe through the bathroom door. I heard Chloe emerge and go into her mum's bedroom. There was the murmur of voices. No doubt she was telling her mum what a bitch I was.

Fighting off the dog was now top of my agenda. He was licking my neck. I went out to the kitchen and gave him a ginger biscuit, which he carried off to his basket. As I returned to the sitting room, I heard

Chloe coming downstairs. Her face was strange and mottled. She didn't look me in the eye.

'Which is my coffee?' she asked.

'Oh, sorry,' I said. 'I didn't realise you wanted one.' I jumped up and headed for the kitchen. Anything to be out of her company for a split second.

'It's OK,' she said. 'I don't want one anyway.'

There was a horrid tense silence. Chloe went and sat on a chair by her mum's little table, as far away from me as possible. She pretended to be sorting some papers.

Matthew was still trying to write the essay, resting his paper on the movie stars book, on his knees. I suddenly realised that unless I did something, we were going to be stuck in this wordless torment for eternity.

'Don't worry about doing that now!' I trilled. Matthew looked up, puzzled.

'But I've only just started it,' he droned. 'I'm not even halfway through my first short-term aspiration.' He sounded disappointed.

'Tell you what!' I beamed. 'Why don't you do that writing project at home? It'll be easier to concentrate. And we'll not charge you for the full hour.'

'Yeah,' said Matthew. 'And I'd be able to print off

236

some photos from my archive. My second medium-term aim is to cross Northern Canada with a dog team. I've got some quite good photos of the Arctic wastes.'

'Brilliant!' I cried, trying not to sound hysterical. 'I can't wait to see them!'

Then Matthew packed away his various papers in his briefcase and stood up.

'What about your coffee?' I asked.

'Er . . . I don't really like coffee, to be honest,' he said. 'Or tea. Maybe we could have a session some-time about which beverages to ask for?'

'Spring water,' I said briskly. I stood up, and Chloe also rose and kind of pointed at the door in a way which was far from gracious. It was the same gesture she uses to Geraint sometimes when he has been a bit of a nuisance.

'What about the payment?' asked Matthew awk-wardly. 'Will you bill me at the end of the month?'

'Of course,' I said. 'We'll be in touch soon about your next session. And the Ball, of course.'

I held out my hand. Matthew made a huge effort and squeezed it slightly. After that, he turned his back on me and followed Chloe out to the hall. Rarely have I felt more relieved to part from anybody. If only he would take Chloe with him and disappear for ever.

I carried the rejected cups of coffee back to the kitchen, and tipped them down the sink. Fran arrived, wearing a blouse decorated with green monkeys.

'Zoe,' she said. 'About you having nobody to go to the Ball with ... would you like me to do a tarot reading for you?'

I jumped at the offer. It would mean I wouldn't have to speak to Chloe. I knew I couldn't talk to Chloe without continuing our row, and I didn't see how we could manage it with her mum there. So Fran and I went to her special astrological table and sat down.

Chloe returned from banishing Matthew into the twilight just as Fran was getting out her cards. She looked exceedingly grumpy.

'Maybe you could whip up a little supper for us, darling,' said Fran. Chloe scowled, went off to the kitchen and shut the door with just the hint of a bad-tempered slam. Fran ignored this. She was totally focused on her tarot ritual.

'Hello, darlings!' Fran whispered to her cards. She shuffled them, then asked me to pick seven, and laid them out in a strange magicky pattern on the carpet tablecloth.

Geraint stirred on the hearthrug, got up laboriously, wandered over to us and started to lick my knees.

'Take Geraint out for a walk, Chloe!' called her mum. 'I don't want his vibes disturbing my energies! And don't forget the pooper-scooper!'

Chloe emerged from the kitchen, looking daggers. 'I've only just started to make the supper!' she snapped.

'Don't argue,' said her mum, staring at the cards. Chloe heaved a massive self-pitying sigh, put Geraint's lead on, and went out.

'Now, Zoe . . .' said Fran, staring at the cards I'd chosen. 'Let's see . . . there's a misunderstanding with a male person.' Not exactly earth-shaking in its originality, but nevertheless, true. It must be Oliver!

'You have to tell him what's really what, Zoe,' she went on, peering at me between her thick hanks of grey hair. 'Otherwise it'll just be delays, suspicions and misunderstandings.' She pointed at a card with a picture of a sad-faced moon. 'The message seems clear,' said Fran. I was surprised. 'Sort out this misunderstanding with the young man, and he will ask you to the Ball. Yes?'

'Oh,' I said, faint at the idea of Oliver asking me to the Ball. 'Wow!' I didn't have the heart to tell her that Oliver would never – *never* – ask me to the Ball, not in a million years. My aim was far more modest. I just had to try to stop him thinking I was an idiot.

Then Chloe's mum talked about deals involving large amounts of money, and how I had to be careful because the Queen of Hearts was involved. (Tamsin, clearly). After that Fran said the power of the reading began to wane. Or maybe she was getting bored with it.

However, we ended in quite a mellow mood. The session with Fran had distracted me and calmed me down. But when, moments later, Chloe returned, her face was so stony I could see she was still sunk in deep hatred of me. She was carrying one of Geraint's gigantic turds wrapped in a plastic bag.

'Would you like to stay to supper, Zoe?' asked Chloe's mum. Mesmerised by the turd, I thought perhaps not. I couldn't face any more of Chloe's sulks. I knew our blazing row had only been postponed, so the atmosphere would be poisonous.

I was halfway home, and mentally rehearsing a scene with Oliver, when my mobile rang.

'Hi,' said a deep sexy voice. 'This is Matt.' It's strange how I never noticed how deep and sexy his voice was when he was actually in the room.

'Uh, sorry to disturb you,' said Matt. 'I was just wondering . . . do you think I should have an earring?'

'Not for the present,' I said. 'Just concentrate on the smile, the handshake and the colour brown.'

'OK,' said Matthew, 'just one other thing. This, uh – going to the Ball with Chloe . . . will you be there?'

'Yes,' I said, 'of course.'

'Do you have a partner?' asked Matthew bluntly. Maybe he had a friend who would like to escort me? I was certain that no friend of Matthew could ever be anything but dullsville.

'Yes,' I said. 'I'm going with Nigel.' Matt need not know, right now, that Nigel was not a boy, but a spot on my chin.

'Oh,' Matt said, sounding a bit disappointed. 'I just thought – really uh, I sort of feel I hardly know Chloe, you see, and I was just thinking, uh – to be honest, I'd much rather go with you.'

28

WEDNESDAY 6.03 P.M.

Emotional blackmail, anyone?

While obviously pleased that Matthew preferred me to Chloe, the thought of spending a whole evening in his company made me want to pack my bags and head straight to the airport. I told Matthew what a terrific person Chloe was, ignoring, for a moment, my current loathing of her. I assured him it was an honour that she'd asked him to the Ball. He accepted the idea politely, but you could tell he was unconvinced.

'Just one other thing,' said Matthew. 'Do you think I should cut my hair?'

I told him to keep on slicking it back for the time being, and promised to give it some thought. I was beginning to tire of being a life coach. Having to spend time thinking about Matthew's hair was not so much a style project, more a severe sentence.

Back home, everything was low-key. Mum and Dad were snuggled up on the sofa, watching a documentary about the Egyptians. Supper was help-yourself to a tired salad that had been in the fridge for three days already. I wasn't hungry, actually. I felt kind of sick after my confrontation with Chloe.

I went upstairs, lay down on my bed and stared moodily at the ceiling. Suddenly my mobile rang. I grabbed it. It was Chloe and she was clearly ballistic.

'So!' she snapped. 'What was all that about? You were completely out of order! What's the matter with you?'

'No!' I was so furious, I jumped up off my bed and began pacing the room. 'What's the matter with *you*? That's the issue. I'm just totally sick of the way you let me down all the time.'

'What do you freakin' *mean*?' screamed Chloe. 'Let you down? Like, when?'

'Like, always!' I yelled. 'We go to the Toilethead concert – you go off with Beast.'

'They gave me a lift home!' shouted Chloe. 'I sprained my ankle, remember?'

'We could have taken a taxi! You just abandoned me!'

'I so did not! We offered you a lift and you just went all moody!'

'I did *not* go moody. I just didn't want to spend any time with those morons! And then you wouldn't come to babysit with me – instead you had to go waltzing off with Beast again. Then when it went pear-shaped you came crawling back and got me into big trouble with the Normans!'

'I've already apologised for that!'

'You never contribute! I'm always the one who has to answer the door, talk to the androids, whatever. Then when Beast rings, you run out like an idiot and have a shouting match with him upstairs while I'm trying to deal with Matthew.'

'Look, I was telling Beast to get lost! You can't have it both ways, Zoe! You're so freakin' judge-mental!'

'Then you come barging in again and ask Matthew to the Ball, without even discussing it with me first!' I was determined to get all my resentment out now, without getting side-tracked by her arguments. 'I never know what you're going to do next. You just do or say whatever comes into your head. And if Beast is in the picture, you just don't give a toss about me. I get no support. You're never there for me. I'm, like, totally irrelevant to your life!'

'Don't be such a stupid bitch!' screeched Chloe. 'How can you be irrelevant to my life when I just lent you my entire year's savings – £225! Call that No Support? What more do you want? I don't have to put up with this.'

And she rang off. I felt sicker than ever. OK, I'd got it all off my chest – all the irritation I'd been feeling recently. But she had produced the trump card. That loan. All her money, handed over to me, without a moment's hesitation. A huge wave of guilt washed over me. OK, Chloe could be a bit of an airhead, unpredictable and ditsy. But could anybody have been more generous to me in my hour of need?

Immediately I called her back to apologise. But her mobile was switched off. I rang her landline. No reply. Her mum must have gone out, and Chloe wasn't picking up. I didn't leave a message. I couldn't think of the words. I didn't sleep too well that night. I dreamed my teeth were falling out.

Walking to school next day seemed like a huge effort. I was light-headed and my legs felt hollow and weak. Would Chloe ever speak to me again? Would she ask for her money back? As I reached the gate, I saw her waiting. She headed straight for me. I flinched a little. What was coming? A right hook? She grabbed my wrist.

'I'm really, really sorry, Zoe,' she said, her eyes full of tears. 'I was a bitch. I've been a total pain recently and I promise I'll try and do better.'

'I'm sorry,' I mumbled guiltily. 'I was totally out of order. I've just got so irritable recently. Sorry, Chloe.' We fell into each other's arms and had a massive hug. 'You can have the money back right away if you like,' I murmured into her ear.

'No, no!' she pulled away, smiling. 'I want Tam to have it! She's in a fix and I can help! She's always been so nice to me.'

We strolled off, arm in arm. The sun felt unusually shiny. The sky was fabulously blue. We were never going to row again. Well, not this week, anyway.

'So what's the situation between you and Oliver?' asked Chloe.

How could I explain to Chloe the full intricate horror of my misunderstanding with Oliver? It would take all day. Besides, Jess and Flora were coming up.

'It's complicated,' I said. 'I'll explain at lunch.'

'Chloe,' said Jess. 'We've heard you can do somer-saults. Is that true?'

'Well . . . yes,' said Chloe. Though useless at ball games and swimming, she can mysteriously do cart-wheels and stuff.

'Well, we're doing an assembly next week and it kind of needs somebody to turn somersaults in it,' Jess went on. 'Any chance you could be that person? No pressure. Just, if you don't, children will die in Africa because of you.'

Chloe started talking about the assembly with Flora and Jess. I went off into a kind of daydream. I was rehearsing a speech. At break I would go to the sixth-form area and hang around until Oliver appeared. Then, with a couple of graceful and care-free sentences, I would explain everything. I would be enchanting.

'Oh, hi, Oliver!' I would call, as if it was such a *surprise* to see him at this moment. In fact, as if I'd briefly forgotten about his very existence. 'How's it going?' And then, after he'd told me how it was going, I'd say, 'Listen, I'm sorry about the misunder-standing about the farm. I've been the victim of an elaborate practical joke. My parents brought me up to believe we lived on a farm, but I've recently discovered that we do, in fact, live in a perfectly ordinary house like everybody else.

'And when my mum puts on her smart suit and picks up her briefcase, she's not, as she always said, going off to milk the cows, but apparently, to investigate insurance claims. My parents invented this ludicrous story because they were so embarrassed about the insurance business that they were afraid I might run away from home. But, you know. I quite like my house anyway. Er . . . *where do you live, by the way?*'

And then, when he'd told me where he lived, I'd go round after dark and pick a bit of his hedge. And I'd tuck it in my bra, next to my heart, and never take it out for the rest of my life, even if it was quite prickly.

Chloe went off with Flora and Jess to demonstrate her somersaults in the hall. I just leaned against the fence. Hundreds of kids were milling about. But none of them was Oliver. I never see him when I'm looking for him. Then, when I least expect it, he appears. I read somewhere that ghosts are a bit like that.

'Hi! Zoe!' I looked round. It was Toby (also looking round – we've often discussed going on a diet together). He was eating a packet of crisps.

'Crisps before 9 a.m.?' I said, in a cross, lecturing

kind of voice. 'What did you have for breakfast, may I ask?'

'Nothing,' said Toby. 'This is my breakfast. I don't count muesli.'

'How are you, anyway, my dear?' I started in on the old-lady voice we sometimes use. But Toby didn't pick up on it today. In fact, he sighed.

'Oh . . .' he said, tipping the last crumbs of crisps into his mouth and wiping his lips on his hand. 'You know . . . rubbish.'

'Why rubbish?' I cried indignantly. Toby's supposed to cheer me up. He's usually *relentlessly* optimistic. 'Listen, Tobe! You're my hero! That money you lent me has literally saved my sister's life!' Toby looked surprised.

'Uh . . . ?'

'Well, not *literally* literally,' I went on. 'Although yeah! Maybe *literally* literally! Because when she first rang me to tell me how fed up she was, she was walking down by the river in the rain, in the dark! She could easily have thrown herself in, and now she's as happy as anything – thanks to you, Tobes!'

'Well,' said Toby. 'Good.' And he burped. It was quite a sad burp, though, and he still looked rather down in the mouth.

'So what's the problem?' I asked. He shrugged.

'Fergus says we might as well sell our Earthquake Ball tickets,' said Toby. 'Nobody's ever going to want to come with us.'

'Rubbish!' I shrieked. 'Toby, you've gotta go! Everyone's going! Don't be such a pillock – of course somebody will go with you!'

'Who?' said Toby simply, shrugging. His eyes were huge, and fixed on me like two luminous blue-and-white planets.

Suddenly, in my secret heart of hearts, I felt a sickening jolt. Toby hadn't said anything, but weirdly I had this sense that because he'd lent me all his money, I sort of had to go to the Ball with him *myself*! Noooooooo! Toby was a mate, and a good mate. The best. But the Earthquake Ball was so *not* the event to go to just with your mate.

If I thought I had to go with Toby I would literally die. Well, not *literally* literally.

'Somebody will snap you up!' I yelled. 'You're gorgeous! You're both amazingly fun guys! Go out and hunt down a couple of blondes!' This was a code way of making sure he never thought about me and Chloe as possible partners, because I'm mousy and Chloe's a redhead.

'We went out so-called hunting last night,' said Toby. 'We went bowling. Even the most munting girls there wouldn't look at us. They said we were gay.'

'Well, what do you expect from girls who haunt the bowling alley?' I asked, swiftly ignoring the fact that I've had some of the best evenings of my life there. 'Try the pool. Or the skating rink. Or the Dolphin Cafe. That waitress in the Dolphin fancies you. She's always flirting when we go in there.'

'She flirts with anything alive,' said Toby sadly. 'I saw her last week flirting with a tomato.'

The bell rang for registration. In the distance I could see Fergus approaching. Chloe is literally (yes, this time *literally*) petite – no more than five foot two in her shoes, and Fergus is at least *half a head* shorter. For one brief horrible moment a vision flashed before my eyes of Chloe in a fab green ballgown and Fergus tagging along beside her in a tuxedo. I'm sorry to be smallist, but it looked completely *ridiculous*. As if he was her adopted orphan son or something.

'Who are you going with?' asked Toby suddenly. I almost jumped right out of my skin. On the one hand, Toby's question looked like a simple, straight-forward enquiry.

On the other, it felt like a red-hot dangerous inter-rogation that might lead directly to the worst thing he could ever possibly say, i.e., *'Why don't you come with me?'*

'It's kind of a secret,' I said, and winked at him. Or tried to wink. But I was so nervous, my eyelid sort of stuck down (too much mascara, also, I admit.) Instead of looking sporty and playful I appeared, for a moment, only sinister and deranged.

'Oh,' said Toby. 'I wish I had a secret partner lined up. Very glamorous and exciting, my dear!' He tried, at last, for the old-lady voice, but got it slightly wrong. He just wasn't in the mood, poor Tobe.

'Don't worry, Toblerone,' I squeezed his arm, but only briefly, and in a totally unsexy kind of way, 'you *shall* go to the Ball! Leave it to me.'

'Will you be my fairy godmother, then?' asked Toby with the ghost of a smile.

'I certainly jolly well will, my dear!' I assured him in my old lady's voice. Chloe and Fergus joined us, and we went off to registration. They were talking about a film. I wasn't really listening. My mind was reeling.

What had I done? Not only did I have to find a partner for me, but I now had to find one for Toby too. And possibly Fergus.

But first I had to find Oliver and explain why I'd said I lived on a farm. Just how complicated could a day be? I was exhausted already.

29

THURSDAY 11.03 A.M.

Swept off my feet by his roller-coaster

At break, I heaved a deep sigh and tried to summon my few pathetic shreds of courage.

'I have to go and confront Oliver,' I told Chloe. 'I have to explain that misunderstanding we had.'

'Oh . . . right,' said Chloe. She was smiling and trying to look positive and supportive, but I could tell she couldn't quite remember what I was talking about. 'I've got to go and see Dingle anyway, to get that work I missed on Tuesday. Then it's maths.' We're in separate sets for maths, for reasons which must remain private.

'I'll see you at lunchtime, then,' I said, and trudged off towards my appointment with doom.

I'd got my speech all ready. Well, it was hardly a

speech. More a sort of brief aside. It went like this: 'I'm sorry about the misunderstanding about the farm. I was telling Donut I lived on a farm because he was hitting on me and I wanted him to think I lived way way out in the sticks, so I'd, like, *never* be available to go out anywhere.' It sounded so lame, but it was, in fact, just the plain old truth. So if I only managed to say this to Oliver, at least it wouldn't rebound horribly on me and cause me loads of extra hassle.

I walked towards the sixth-form area, my heart starting to beat like a drum. The sixth form are based on the first floor, at the far side of the school, where the corridor turns into a sort of open balcony thing overlooking the field. As I reached this point, I glanced down. It was quite a sunny spring-like day and crowds of people had gone down on to the field. And there, talking to some guys, was Oliver!

He had his back to me, but of course I recognised it immediately. Just the sight of his shoulders, a hundred metres away, was enough to send all my nerves and arteries into some kind of deranged dance. I turned round, raced back along the corridor, down some steps and out on to the school's back terrace – and down some more steps on to the field.

By now I was panting unattractively. Whoa! Big mistake that was. I should have strolled here. How could I look casual and offhand, as if I'd just bumped into him, if I was bright red and gasping for breath? I'd have to say I was desperately seeking Chloe.

Now I was surrounded by crowds, and I couldn't see Oliver at all. I pushed my way through gangs of random people. Occasionally someone said, 'Hi Zoe!' But I just waved and pulled an *I'm busy* face, and pressed on. I reached the edge of the crowd eventually, and looked around. Still no sign of Oliver. I panicked. And then I double-panicked. For strolling towards me looking mad, bad and dangerous was none other than Beast and his moronic sidekick, Donut.

'Hi, darlin'!' he said, and suddenly he was right up close, invading my personal space with his strange glittering eyes. 'Looking for somebody? Who's the lucky guy? Could it be me? If not, why not?'

I hesitated. For a moment I was tempted to say I was looking for Oliver. But I *so* wanted to keep the Oliver part of my life separate from the Beast 'n' Donut part of my life.

'You're out of breath, babe!' Beast went on. He was actually stroking my arm, now, the animal! 'Hey!

Relax! Calm down.'

'I am relaxed!' I snapped, in hyper-stress. 'I am deeply deeply calm!'

Beast laughed.

'I love the way you talk! Don't you love the way she talks, Doh?' Donut nodded eagerly. To please his master he would be prepared to love the way I spat.

'Tell you what, though, babe,' he said, 'you're not very fit, are you? I don't mean *not fit*, like, not good-looking. To be honest I've always thought you were one of the best-looking girls in the school. I mean, *not fit*, like, needing a fitness programme and a personal trainer. And I'm the man for the job.'

'You are so *not*!' I retorted, though it was really hard to stand up to him. Somehow he slithered his way round you like a snake. 'If I ever decide to do a fitness programme, I'm quite capable of organising it myself, thanks very much.'

'Anybody ever told you what sweet little dimples you got, Zoe?' he said, grinning practically into my face. I was furious. How dare Beast hit on me here, on the school field? How dare he hit on me anywhere?

'My dimples,' I said coldly, 'are nothing compared to Chloe's freckles, which you must have noticed, as you spent so much time with her recently.'

'Ahhh, your little friend,' breathed Beast, putting his arm round my shoulders. 'Tell you what, Zoe, she's a cracker. But I think I must have done something to upset her, cos she won't speak to me now. And to tell you the truth, she's not really my type. I like a girl with a bit of flesh on her. Something cuddly. Something to grab hold of.' And his big beastly fingers closed around my upper arm, squeezing my special store of flab till it almost hurt.

'Thanks for pointing out that I am technically overweight!' I sneered. 'Such wonderful manners!'

'You're not overweight, babe!' he grinned. 'You're perfect! Overweight, my arse! You're as light as a freakin' feather – look!' Suddenly he kind of bent down slightly, and before I knew what was happening, he had hoisted me up on to his shoulder and was wheeling me round. Round and round and round. The field, the sky, the school, all flashed past in a madly whirling horizon.

I screamed. Everybody laughed. I held on tight to Beast's jacket, because though this mad whirling circus performance was the last thing on earth I wanted to be doing, I certainly didn't want to crash to the ground and end up brain damaged.

Beast was horribly strong. He's a rugby player and they are always tossing each other about like bags of laundry.

'Put me down!' I screamed. 'Put me down!' And then I got kind of hysterical, and started laughing madly. It wasn't that I was enjoying myself – quite the contrary. I have never enjoyed a moment less. But I just felt so totally helpless, I kind of freaked out. My body was trapped: laughing seemed all it could do. It was a painful kind of laughing, though. Quite close to crying, in fact.

Faces of people nearby loomed and vanished. It was like being on a roundabout at the fair. I began to feel sick. Then suddenly, out of the crowd, Oliver's face flashed past. Oliver was watching!

'Put me down!' I roared unattractively. 'I'm going to be sick!'

That did the trick. Beast lowered me to the ground. I wasn't actually sick, but my head was spinning. I had to stand ultra-still for a while and hold on to my head until the field stopped spinning, bucking and rocking.

I looked round. Oliver had vanished. A blonde girl had come up to Beast and was, apparently, demanding the same treatment, as if it was some kind of joyride. He was busy chatting her up. It was as if I'd never existed. My enchanting dimples and lovable flab were on the scrap heap – thank God. I wouldn't have to ask Chloe ever again what had happened between her and Beast. I'd experienced it myself, in two minutes flat.

My legs began to feel normal again. I limped off quietly into the crowds. My stomach was still queasy, though. But it wasn't the vertigo. It wasn't physical. It was the knowledge that Oliver had now seen me three times: once, with Donut fingering my earrings; once, with my arms flung around Toby, and now, being tossed about by Beast as if I was some kind of plaything, and I'd been laughing like a drunken slapper.

30

THURSDAY 7.12 P.M.

A touching offer in the bathroom . . .

A depression settled over me. I was deep in the glooms. My life was in ruins. Oliver would probably never speak to me again. There was nobody to take me to the Earthquake Ball. Matthew would be taking Chloe – and despite my efforts he was still technically a robot. And he'd be expecting to meet my partner Nigel, in order, possibly, to challenge him to a duel over me.

Worse, I was going to fail utterly as fairy god-mother to Toby and Fergus. They might as well invest in a couple of scarecrows as partners. Even a mediocre scarecrow would be better looking than any girl I was likely to be able to recruit at this late stage.

'By the way, Zoe,' said Mum at supper, 'when's

that school trip, again?'

'What school trip?' I asked listlessly, from the depths of my tragic despair.

'The all-male *Hamlet* in Russian,' said Mum. My heart gave a massive, salad-threatening lurch. Oh, *that* school trip!

'It's next week – but, uh, excuse me,' I said, leaping up in terror and running out of the room in what I hoped was a carefree but trustworthy manner.

'Come back!' she said. 'You haven't finished your salad!'

'Just going to the loo!' I trilled, thundering up the stairs. Horrors! I had so many reasons to be desperate, I couldn't even remember them all at once! I had totally forgotten about *Hamlet*. How was I going to get myself out of that one?

Sometimes the bathroom is the only place where you can chill out. I decided to forget my woes by losing myself in a trashy magazine. I was halfway through a page devoted to Celebrity Lovebites when my phone rang. It was Fergus. Bizarre! And even more bizarre if he'd known where I was sitting.

'Fergy baby!' I addressed him. 'What's the story?'

'OKOK,' said Fergus in his usual quick-fire jittery style. 'ICan'tManage MuchButICanDoFifty. OK?'

'Fifty?' I was briefly puzzled. Part of my brain was still involved with Celebrity Lovebites, and to be honest, wanting to take the subject a lot further.

'FiftyQuid,' said Fergus. 'I'llBringItToSchool Tomorrow. OK?'

'Fergus!' I cried. 'You're the lovechild of the goddess Venus!'

'Ugh!Ugh! ISureAsHellHopeNot,' said Fergus. 'SeeYouTomorrow. Bye!'

Dear little Fergus! Ransacking his piggy bank! Prizing his little pennies out and putting them in a sweet little envelope just to help his rather sad friend, Yours Truly! I was thinking of Fergus with great affection as I wiped my bum. Although to be honest I'm not sure he would ever want to know that.

I washed my hands with endless care, just to waste a bit more time, and then went back downstairs to pick at the last few shreds of salad. Mum was now busy arguing with Dad about whether they were going away for a weekend sometime soon. Good. This meant she had, temporarily at least, forgotten about my 'school trip'.

'But I love Tenby!' Dad was saying.

'You're such an old stick-in-the-mud,' complained Mum. 'I want to whisk you away to Nice for a romantic break by the Med!'

'Who's going to look after little Zoe?' asked Dad, putting on a *pity for the tragic orphan* kind of face.

'She can go to Chloe's, like she always does!' Mum assured him.

I shovelled down the last of my supper and then swiftly cleared away the dishes. I was feeling slightly better since Fergus's call. He had reminded me how lucky I was to have buddies like him. I just *had* to find him a partner for the Earthquake Ball. I might have to go down to New Look and bribe a tiny but cute starlet as she emerged from the changing rooms.

I went back upstairs and entered Tam's room. I lay on her bed and sent her a text. **HAVE GOT BIG BUCKS FOR YOU. FUND CURRENTLY STANDS AT AROUND £692. I THINK THAT MIGHT HAVE TO BE IT THOUGH. LV, Z X**

Immediately a text whizzed back: **YOU BEAUT, ZOE! I'LL COME HOME THIS WEEKEND AND COLLECT IT. OH WHOOPEE!**

I was glad she was pleased, but I wasn't sure about that '*Oh whoopee*' business. She sounded a bit rampant. As if she might just grab my friends' dosh, race off to the mall, and blow it all on glass slippers and golden coaches. I looked around her room.

Everywhere it seemed there was some kind of evidence against her.

Sparkly scarves hanging from her hat stand. The hat stand itself (antique pine – a junk shop purchase.) Something made of ostrich feathers. I don't much like feathers. They're OK on birds, but I feel that's where they should stay. I stared rather moodily at her guitar, amp and keyboard. A couple of years ago Tam had toyed with the idea of being a rock star.

On her noticeboard there were lots of photos of her at various ages. Some of the photos had me in as well. I would always be just standing there like a sack of sand, grinning nerdily at the camera. But Tam would be striking a pose, all the time. Hand on hip, pouting lip, pulling a 'hideous' face but somehow still effortlessly Hollywood ... you know the sort of thing.

I felt a bit tired, turned over towards the wall and came face to face with her old teddy bear, Captain. His gloomy old snout was up close to mine. He's a miserable old bear, to be honest, but then you'd be miserable if your mistress had gone off to uni and left you at home. She told him it was because his arms have a tendency to fall off and she didn't want him to get damaged. But Captain knew it was because she didn't want him to be staring disapprovingly at her as she had all that wonderful fun with her friends.

'Captain,' I said, just to pass the time, 'you smell of old tears. But you ain't seen nothing yet.' I thought it might be a considerate act, if I felt a crying fit coming on (and didn't I just!) to offer it to Captain rather than my own bear, Bruce, who is smiley, fluffy, and possibly gay. Bruce certainly wouldn't mind being passed over for Captain once in a while. He's so laid back, he won't even sit up properly. If you try to sit him upright, he just topples sideways with a louche grin on his face.

I went into my bedroom. Bruce was sprawling on his back, smiling at the ceiling. I'm certainly going to take him with me if I ever go to uni. He's such a party animal.

I opened the wardrobe door. This was where I'd stashed the big bucks. There were two boxes in there – a small one full of clothes I'm certainly going to donate to charity, and a big one half-full of clothes I *might* donate. On top was a sequinned boob tube from my mum's old college days. I scrabbled about under this pile until I felt the magic envelope. I rather furtively got it out and peeped inside. So many notes! So much money! It was wonderful, but also kind of scary. I closed the envelope again and tucked it safely away, underneath all the 'Clothes I Might Donate'. Then I closed the wardrobe door, and joined Bruce on the bed.

I was halfway through our first cuddle when my mobile rang again. What was this? Tam reporting that she'd already got through my first £100 by setting up a tab and treating everyone in the college bar to a flagon of champagne? Oh no – it was Chloe.

'Zoe!' she sounded deep in crisis, as usual. 'I can't go to the Ball with Matthew! I've been thinking about it and I was mad to ask him. It was only because I'd just had a row with Beast. Please, please get me out of this! Ring him and tell him I'm ill! I know I'm being useless and horrid again but please, just do this one small thing for me and I promise, from now on I'll be fabulous and help you out with all the tough stuff!'

I had to smile. 'No listen, Chloe,' I said gently. 'This is the perfect opportunity for you to start doing the tough stuff right now. You asked him to the Ball, so it's got to be you who dumps him. OK?' I knew if I rang Matthew and told him Chloe was ill, he'd ask me to go with him instead – Nigel or no Nigel.

'Oh no! I couldn't dump him!' said Chloe. 'Poor

Matthew! But, Zoe, how can I go with him? He's weird.'

'Sleep on it,' I advised her. 'Give it twenty-four hours, and if you're still horrified at the thought, we'll think of something then.'

'Come round my house tomorrow night after school,' said Chloe. 'It'll be our last chance to sort something out. Frankly I'm so sick of this Ball business I'd willingly go down with food poisoning just to avoid it.'

It was indeed a tempting thought.

'Well, come round mine,' I said. 'It's my dad's night to cook. You never know, we might get lucky.'

31

FRIDAY 4.55 P.M.

Disastrous timing . . .

It was an averagely unpleasant school day. I didn't glimpse Oliver anywhere. I kind of knew he'd be going to the Ball with the long-legged girl. All I asked was that he didn't actually snog her in front of me.

Nigel had revved up into one of his madly pulsating crescendos. Everywhere I went, I felt my spot was leading the way and emitting blinding rays like a miner's lamp.

Chloe had spent the whole day obsessing about Matthew. Half the time she'd reconciled herself to going with him, and half the time she wanted me to go round to his house and slip a bit of germ warfare through the letter box. I hadn't had the heart to tell

269

her he'd said he'd rather go with me, anyway. If I'd said that, Chloe would have yelled, 'Well, you go with him, then! The perfect solution!'

No way would I go to the ball with Matthew. He was an android. It would be unprofessional, anyway. I was his life coach. He'd rung me up a few more times – once to ask if he should have a tattoo, once to get my advice about what sort of shoes to wear to the Ball. I was beginning to think I should charge him for these calls.

Toby and Fergus had tried and failed to sell their tickets. They had evidently decided that, as a fairy godmother, I was crap. I had to admit there were no magic spells in the cupboard.

'It's all right for them anyway,' I sighed as we trudged back to my place. 'Boys can just go to the Ball in gangs without looking sad and unloved.'

Chloe stopped in her tracks. She went pale. She went red. She sort of clutched her stomach. I hoped she wasn't going to be sick.

'Oh my God!' she said. 'Oh my God! My God! That's it!'

'What's what?' I enquired nervously.

'We go with them!' spluttered Chloe. 'But as *boys*! We dress as boys! We go as a boys' gang with

Fergus and Toby!'

Feverishly I swept Chloe into my arms. 'You beaut!' I screeched. 'You babe! You Einstein! You've cracked it! Re-sult!'

And locked in a ferocious hug, we wheeled round and round and round on the pavement, scattering school books out of our bags, in a frenzy of celebration.

Moments later, while Chloe picked up the books, I texted Toby: **PROB SOLVED! YOU SHALL GO TO THE BALL! AND WITH VERY UNUSUAL PARTNERS. RING ME NOW!** But Toby didn't ring me, and when I rang him, his phone went straight to voicemail. I was so frustrated and desperate to talk to him I stared at my phone all the way home and tried to force it to ring by the sheer power of thought.

Chloe had texted her mum to say she'd be staying at my place, because this amazing breakthrough was going to take us all evening, and most of tomorrow, to organise.

'I'll ring the fancy dress hire place,' she said. 'God! I hope they've got a tiny tuxedo just big enough for a Hobbit, because if they haven't, I'm stuffed.'

'Right!' I said, racing into the kitchen and grabbing the phone directory. 'You find the number – and we must ring Toby and Fergus on their landlines and tell them we're going as an all-male gang.'

'Hey, Zoe!' came a voice all of a sudden, out of the sitting room. 'What's going on? Some kind of crisis?'

It was Tamsin! She looked as if she'd been dozing on the sofa. She stood in the doorway, a bit sleepy and crumpled, and held out her arms. I bounded down the stairs and gave her a massive hug.

'Love you!' she whispered.

'Love you!' I responded.

'The dress-hire place closes at seven!' shouted Chloe from the kitchen. 'So I'll ask them to put some things aside for us for tomorrow morning!'

'Dress hire?' said Tam, cocking an inquisitive eyebrow.

'It's for the Earthquake Ball!' I said. 'It's tomorrow!'

'Always *so* last minute, Zoe!' laughed Tam. 'Don't spend a fortune hiring anything, though – look what I've brought.'

I went into the sitting room. There was a really huge suitcase in there, on wheels.

'You should have heard the taxi driver curse!' said Tamsin, giggling as she heaved the case on to its side and unzipped it. Inside was a huge kind of lasagne of clothing. Fabulous dresses – some I recognised, some I'd never seen before. Sparkly, satin, sequinned, the lot.

'I'm going to take them to that vintage shop in the high street,' she said. 'I'm sure Dixie will give me a good price. After all, I've been one of her best customers in the past.'

'You're selling them?' I was amazed, but also reassured. Tam is normally such a hoarder.

'Well, I've got to,' she said, in a confidential tone. 'Because of you-know-what. But you can have your pick for the Ball, first.'

'Thanks, but no thanks!' I grinned. 'We won't need dresses for the Ball, because we're going as boys. With tuxedos and everything.'

'Wow! Excellent!' said Tam, but she looked preoccupied. She looked around furtively and dropped her voice to a whisper. 'Listen, Zoe – I hate to seem kind of grasping, but do you think you could give me the muns now, while Mum's out? She'll be back in a minute – she's just gone shopping. Dad's been excused cooking tonight and Mum's going to bring a takeaway back.'

'Where's Dad now?' I asked, listening for sounds upstairs.

'I think he's in the middle of some fiendish bit of web design,' said Tam. 'He had a cup of tea with me when I first arrived, but then he went back upstairs and said he'd got a nasty little glitch he had to iron out. But his door's closed and Freddie Mercury is doing major decibels.'

Dad always listens to Queen when he's wrestling with some kind of computer problem.

Chloe joined us in the hall. 'Tamsin!' she yelled. 'How are you?'

'Chloe!' yelled Tamsin, giving her a major hug. 'You look fabulous! And thank you so very very much for *you know what*! You're an absolute angel!'

'It's fine,' said Chloe. 'Anything to help, you know . . .'

'So . . .' Tam seemed to want to change the subject. Understandably. 'So you guys have got the Ball sorted?'

'Yeah.' Chloe grinned. 'Although we must ring Matthew, Zoe, and tell him I've got the flu.'

'We can't tell him that,' I objected. I knew he would then ask *me*.

'I left a message on Toby's voicemail,' Chloe went on, 'saying, "*Relax, it's all sorted.*" '

'The all-male solution is perfect,' I said. I heaved a

big sigh, and cuddled Tam again. It seemed everything was getting sorted at last.

'You smell nice, Tam.' I said. 'What is that
perfume?'

'It's Ralph Lauren,' said Tam, looking at me
guiltily. 'Don't worry, though, it's not new. Tom gave
it to me when we first got together. We're finished
now, though. I dumped him because he was an evil
influence.'

'Evil?' grinned Chloe. 'How, evil?'

'No, OK, I admit it,' said Tam. 'I dumped him
because he was seeing somebody else. But who cares?
I'm better off without him.'

Tam certainly seemed to be in a buoyant mood.
Her eyes sparkled, her face shone, and her smile was
a mile wide.

'You look really happy, Tam,' I said. 'It's brilliant!'

'Well, that's all because of you, little sis,' said Tam.
'You're going to save my life – shall we sort it out
now, quick, before Mum gets back?'

'OK.' I grinned, and all three of us raced upstairs.
'Bohemian Rhapsody' was blasting out from Dad's
study, but the door was firmly closed. We could bank
on the thirty seconds of privacy necessary to hand
over the sacred stash of notes.

We all crowded into my bedroom. It looked tidier than usual. Then I remembered, the cleaner comes on Fridays. I sort of like it looking tidy, but I also love *being* untidy. It wouldn't take me long to create chaos out of order again. I flung open the wardrobe door – and almost fainted.

The box was gone! Both the boxes were gone! The small one containing the clothes I was definitely going to donate to the charity shop, and the big one containing the other stuff I wasn't quite sure about. And I'd hidden the envelope of cash at the bottom of that box! Oh my God! Where had it gone? I couldn't have lost it! I couldn't have lost over £600 – and mostly my friends' money!

I turned in complete shock and horror to Tam and Chloe. I opened my mouth, but no sound came out. I could feel myself going as red as a beetroot, then as pale as death. My heart was performing these odd mad lurching beats. I felt as if I was going to faint.

'Where is it?' said Tam, looking panic-stricken. 'Where did you leave it?'

'In the box!' I found my voice at last, and shrieked. 'There was a box in my wardrobe! Two boxes! Of old clothes I was sorting out! I hid it under there! They've gone!'

Tam was speechless. Chloe went pale and sat down on the bed. I started to shake. I started to whimper.

'Stop it!' said Tam. 'Calm down, Zoe. We can sort this out.'

Downstairs, I heard the sound of Mum's key in the front door.

32

FRIDAY 7.28 P.M.

More blood-curdling surprises . . .

'Don't tell her!' hissed Tam. 'Don't mention the money!'

'But . . .' Chloe hesitated. It was all very well for Tam to say '*don't mention the money*', but it was actually Chloe's money that had disappeared. My blood ran cold. Chloe didn't finish her sentence. She just kind of gulped like a goldfish.

'Hi, honeys, I'm home!' shouted Mum up the stairs. 'Come down and help me unpack and you will be rewarded with an Indian takeaway!' We looked at one another.

'Try and look happy and relaxed!' said Tam, looking about as happy and relaxed as somebody disappearing into a crocodile. We went downstairs, trying to appear merry and skittish, but it was like wearing shocking pink to a funeral.

'Ah! Chloe!' Mum beamed. 'I thought you might be around, so I got some of your favourite – that potato dish. Aloo something-or-other.'

'Thanks!' said Chloe in a rather pale, anguished voice.

Mum didn't notice. She was putting some plates in the oven to warm. 'Typical of Dad,' she grumbled. 'I asked him to warm up the plates ... Unpack that box, will you, Tam? You'll find some of your favourite treats in there.'

'Ooh, fabulous!' trilled Tam, although her voice went a bit too high and sounded on the edge of mad hysteria. Luckily it was drowned out by the clatter of Dad coming downstairs.

'Where's my tandoori chicken?' he boomed in a caveman voice. It all could have been so much fun, really, if only my life wasn't in ruins. And Tam's life, obviously. And Chloe's, too, of course.

'Mum.' I decided to seize the bull by the horns. 'Where are those boxes of clothes that were in the bottom of my wardrobe?'

'Oh, I took them to the charity shop today,' said Mum. 'I had a day off work so I've had a jolly good clear-out. You did say you wanted to get rid of them.'

'Not *all* of them!' I cried, not really able to hide a howl of anguish. 'I was sorting the stuff in the bigger box! I wanted to keep some of it!'

'It's always hard to let things go,' said Mum brightly, in her therapist mode. 'But you'll feel liberated, really, Zoe, once you realise what a lot of space you've got now.'

If only she knew. It's kind of hard to feel liberated when what you've given away is over £600, and it doesn't even belong to you. And all the space is in your wallet, and your friends' wallets, and in your sister's bank account.

'There was stuff in that box I really, really need!' I said, trying to make it sound important, but not too interestingly crucial.

'What stuff?' Mum was still packing things away, as if she couldn't really be bothered to concentrate on my pathetic little drama. That suited me fine. I didn't want her to stand still and stare ruthlessly at me with her beady little lie detectors. But I did need to find out where the boxes had gone.

'Well, to be honest, I hid my diary in that box,' I said, suddenly seeing a way out.

'Oh, well, never mind,' said Mum. 'They probably

haven't even sorted it yet.'

'We can go into town tomorrow, first thing,' said Tam. 'We can be there when they open. I'll go with you, Zoe. Which shop was it, Mum?'

'Oxfam,' said Mum. 'There's a terrible famine in Africa at the moment.'

'Did you say anything about me in this diary?' Dad asked. 'Do I come out of it well? Were my dashing good looks mentioned?'

'Your flab, you mean,' I said. 'Of course I never mention you in my diary, Dad. It's all about boys at school I have a crush on, and sordid stuff like that.'

'Lay the table!' cried Mum, unpacking the pop-padoms with panache. She was doing her best to create a festive atmosphere, but Tamsin, Chloe and I were finding it really hard to think about anything except running away.

'I wonder if they've unpacked it already?' I said, half to myself, as I laid the table.

'Oh, for goodness' sake, Zoe, stop fretting!' snapped Mum. 'I'll ring them first thing in the morning if you like! Nobody's going to be interested in your diary anyway! Now just relax!'

Relax? I could just as soon have eaten my own feet. OK, nobody's interested in a teenage girl's diary. But who isn't interested in £692?

We all sat down and the boxes of Indian food were laid out on the table, on newspaper. We like eating it like that.

'Excuse the rough-and-ready style, Chloe,' said Mum. 'Those plates should be warm enough now.'

'Presentation is everything,' quipped Dad merrily, his usual joke.

'Oh, you should see the way we eat at home,' said Chloe. 'We eat off the floor – practically!' She gave a brave little grin and a shrug, for all the world as if she wasn't unexpectedly bankrupt and looking forward to a summer of No Holiday Whatever except possibly a weekend break under her own bed.

'So, what have you girls got planned for the weekend?' asked Dad, helping himself to a gigantic piece of chicken coated in red tandoori sauce. I usually adore the colours of Indian food as well as the taste, but tonight nothing looked appetising. I felt more than slightly sick – not just in my stomach, all over. Even my eyebrows felt sick.

'It's the Earthquake Ball,' said Chloe. 'Tomorrow night.'

'Oh yes!' said Dad. 'You were having trouble finding partners – did you sort that out?'

'Yeah, it's great,' I said, trying to rouse myself out of my sick coma by forcing myself to talk about something really positive. 'We had so much trouble for ages. We thought we'd never find anybody. We even advertised on a postcard in the supermarket, as you suggested.'

Mum gave Dad a scolding look. 'You suggested they should advertise? For boys?'

'Only in a light-hearted way,' said Dad. 'Not in any serious sense.'

Suddenly I realised the only way out was to ring Matthew and invite him to our all-male gang. Oh no! We had to ring horrid Scott as well, and tell him . . . well tell him *something*.

'Did you find any?' asked Dad, ladling loads of rice on to his plate.

'Well, we did get two replies,' I told him. 'One was a nerd, and one was an android.'

'What other boys are there?' asked Tam. She laughed in a mad, hysterical way.

'So have you got partners, or not?' said Dad, gazing at his dinner with more rapture than I'd ever seen him lavish on Mum.

'The solution is brilliant. We'd always ruled Toby and Fergus out, because they're so immature and stuff, but we've had this great idea,' I said, conveniently ignoring the fact that the idea had, in fact, been Chloe's.

'We're going to go in drag. We dress as boys, and we'll all go together. It'll be the All-Male Earthquake Ball.'

'Where are you getting the tuxedos?' asked Mum.

'I booked a couple,' said Chloe. 'From the fancy-dress-hire place. We can go there after the charity shop.' She gave me a hysterical look. I passed it on to Tam, who choked slightly on a stuffed paratha. The fact was, if our trip to the charity shop drew a blank, there would be no jolly trip to the dress-hire place. We all knew that unless the money was somehow still magically waiting for us at Oxfam, we'd be in the biggest jam in history.

33

FRIDAY 9.05 P.M.

Catastrophe! Another one!

It was so totally and utterly terrifying, thinking of the people in the charity shop sorting through the clothes and then coming to the nice fat envelope stashed away in the bottom . . .

'Zoe!' said Mum, 'you haven't touched your supper!'

'Sorry, sorry!' I said, picking up my fork and trying to look interested. 'I was just making a mental note to ring the android. We must ring him this evening, Chloe.'

'You ring him,' said Chloe, cringing predictably.

'Guess what, Mum,' said Tam. 'I've brought a whole heap of stuff home to sell.' She tried to sound reassuring and mature. 'You know, just to keep the old finances ticking over. I'm going to sell my guitar and my keyboard, too.'

'We bought you that keyboard!' cried Dad indignantly. 'For your fifteenth birthday!'

'Yes, but . . .' Tamsin squirmed slightly. 'I'm never going to be a rock star. I mean, am I? I haven't touched that stuff for more than two years, Dad.'

'Tam's right,' said Mum. 'The guitar and the keyboard are just assets, lying there doing nothing. Sell them if you like, darling – just make sure you get a good price. Pass the dhal, please, dhal-ing!' she said to Dad in a frisky way. They had a silly little laugh at that. I suppose, in another world, it might have been slightly amusing.

Eventually the endless supper was over. Somehow I had managed to swallow most of a very small meal, but I had spread it around my plate a lot to make it look bigger. Food had never seemed so strange. I had only managed to eat some by not thinking about it at all. At the odd moments when I had thought about it for a second by mistake, it had seemed to me that I was swallowing the heads of mice, small pieces of sticking plaster, and Christmas tree decorations.

We escaped upstairs, closed my bedroom door, and put on some music to blot out our conversation.

'What if somebody's taken it?' hissed Chloe. 'What if, when we go in tomorrow, they say they didn't find it?' A cold feeling swept up from the soles of my feet and ended up giving me the chills all around my neck. I could so easily imagine it. It was so obviously what could happen.

'An envelope?' A fat, sinister-looking woman would say. '*No, dear. Sorry. We done those two boxes yesterday, didn't we, Monica, and there wasn't no envelope what we seen, were there?'* Monica would shake her head. She'd have a moustache. They'd both be wearing fabulous strings of pearls and Givenchy perfume, of course.

'I've got to stop fantasising about the women in the charity shop,' I said with a shudder. 'I'm sure they'll all pocket the dosh without a moment's hesitation!'

'Stop it, Zoe!' said Tam. 'Look on the bright side. They probably haven't sorted it yet. It's probably still there, safe as houses. If they have sorted it and found it, they'll realise it was a mistake. People who work in charity shops are good people, Zoe. They'll be keeping it safe until somebody comes in to claim it, right? All we need to do is turn up there tomorrow morning and ask for our money back. We've got to stop panicking and try to relax or we'll never sleep, and then you'll feel terrible and faint at the Ball.'

'Yeah,' said Chloe. She had had recent experience of fainting in public, and I don't suppose she wanted to repeat it. 'You're right. And at least we've got the Ball sorted. It is so brilliant, this going in drag idea. I can't wait to climb into my tux.'

Suddenly my mobe rang. I panicked slightly. There was only so much bad news I could take.

'Hi!' said a deep sexy voice. 'This is Matt. Everything OK for tomorrow night?'

'Oh, hi, Matt,' I said, pulling a face at Chloe and Tam, 'I was just about to ring you. There's been a slight change of plan. We're going as an all-male gang, so you don't have to actually escort Chloe as such. OK?'

'Cool,' said Matt. He sounded relieved. 'See you there, then. Oh, by the way, I forgot to tell you – I'm a Scorpio.'

'Ah, thanks!' I tried to sound professional. 'I'll put it on your file.'

Matt rang off, possibly to try on something brown or practise shaking hands with himself.

'That was Matt,' I informed Chloe and Tam. 'He told me he's a Scorpio.'

'Watch out for his sting, then,' said Tam.

'Nah,' I retorted. 'I'm going to sting him – wait till he sees my bill. Every time he makes a nuisance call, it's an extra fiver.'

We all smiled slightly at this thought. It was kind of on the road to a normal moment. I wasn't feeling quite so sick. In fact, any minute now I might start feeling hungry, and I'd have to creep downstairs and steal a banana.

Suddenly I got a text, and what I read made my blood run cold – for the hundredth time today. It was from Toby:

HI ZO! JUST TO SAY DON'T WORRY YOUR PRETTY LITTLE HEAD ABOUT THAT EARTHQUAKE BALL - FERGUS AND I HAVE GOT PARTNERS LINED UP. KIND OF A LAST-MINUTE THING, BUT SOMETIMES THAT'S THE BEST WAY, ISN'T IT?

34

FRIDAY 10.03 P.M.

I eat my own knuckles in suspense

'They can't do this! They can't do this!' I yelled. 'Toby says they've got partners!'

'Who?' demanded Chloe, her eyes huge with amazement.

'It doesn't say. I'm going to call him right now!'

'Wait!' said Tam. 'Don't say anything stupid.'

I hesitated. What *could* I say? 'Yeah, you're right. What's the point?' I said, my heart suddenly sinking deep, deep into the deepest blue depths of torment. 'They're not available. That's all that matters. We'll have to be an all-male gang on our own.'

'It won't work!' said Chloe, panicking royally as only she knows how. 'We need those guys! On our own we'll just look weird and pervy! And I've reserved the tuxedos and everything! And it was going to be so perfect and funny!' She was right. My mind raced. We had to get Toby and Fergus to go with us. *Had* to.

'I'll think of something in a minute,' I promised. But my mind was disastrously blank.

'What? What?' squealed Chloe, jumping up and down in distress. 'Unless we think of something, we're just going to have to *not go*.'

'Not go?' I screeched at Chloe. 'When I said that a week ago, you said you'd personally strip all the flesh off my body and make a gigantic cheeseburger of me!'

'Well,' said Chloe, looking uncomfortable, 'things have changed. It's only one evening, for God's sake. We don't *have* to be there.'

'Wait, wait, there's no need to give up,' said Tam. 'What other boys are there? You'll have Matt, won't you?'

'It won't work with just Matt,' I said grimly. 'He's too weird, and nobody knows him because he goes to St Kenneth's. He'll only make it worse. We have to have Toby and Fergus. This is *so* ironical. I mean, we've been ruling them out all along because they are so way, way too immature and, well, basically just so

NOT the kind of boys you'd ever take to the Ball. Going as an all-male gang was the perfect way of making it acceptable.'

'Hmm,' said Tam. 'Seems like the tables are turned and it's Toby and Fergus who have to do you a favour.'

'Yeah,' said Chloe. 'Weird!'

I suddenly got an idea. It just might work. OK, it involved major grovelling and went against all my instincts, but it was worth a try.

'Tam, you've got to ring Toby,' I said. 'I can't do this. It has to be, like, someone else.' But I told her what to say. She smiled slightly at the idea.

'I can't stand the tension,' said Chloe. 'I'm going to hide in the bathroom while you make this call, Tam.' And she went out.

Tam got out her phone. It had to be her phone. If it was mine, Toby would know right away that it was one of my cunning plots. Tam dialled Toby's number. I curled up on the bed and rammed my fist into my mouth.

'Hi! Toby?' chirped Tam, sounding wonderfully offhand and cool. 'It's Tam. How are you, young man? Have you been behaving yourself since I went off to uni?' There was a silence while she listened to a bit of Toby's banter. Tam and Toby are great mates. We used to go on camping trips together when we were younger.

'Great! You are such a legend!' laughed Tam, softening him up nicely. (Or so I hoped.) 'Listen, I've got to be quick, because Zoe's in the shower and I don't want her to know I've rung you. Did you realise that she and Chloe cooked up this idea to go to the Ball dressed as boys? As part of an all-male gang? But they need you to be there with them, guys! They've been wanting to ask you for weeks, but they thought you wouldn't want to go with them because they're so nerdy and weird – their words, not mine!' I curled up even more tightly and jammed my fingers in my ears.

There was a silence while Tam listened. 'I know, I know! Well, you know Zoe – she seems confident, but underneath she's really shy.' I could still hear this, unfortunately. Tam was laying it on thick. I was in several kinds of agony. But she was doing a fantastic job. I was so tempted to join Chloe in the bathroom until this painful act was over.

'But listen, Tobe. Is there any chance – I realise it's asking a lot – that you could put these other two girls of yours on hold and join Zoe and Chloe's all-male

293

gang instead?' Then Tam listened for quite a while, grinning and nodding.

'Do you think so? Do you really think so? I mean, I hate to ask, really, it's such a cheek, when you've already got partners, but according to what Zoe said, it was quite a last-minute thing, so I wondered . . . ? OK, OK, fine – talk to you soon, then.' Tam threw her phone on to the bed and grinned at me.

'He's going to call me back,' she said. 'After he's talked to Fergus and the girls.'

'Fingers crossed, then,' I said.

'Fingers, toes, eyes, knees and ankles crossed,' said Tam, crossing her eyes but still somehow failing to look unattractive even for a split second.

I went to get Chloe from the bathroom and explained that Toby was going to ring back.

'He'll never dump those two girls,' said Chloe. 'It's too much to ask. I wonder who they are? Maybe somebody from the year below?'

We sat around in my room basically waiting for Toby to ring back. We started to watch a DVD but nobody was really concentrating. Suddenly my mobe rang. I grabbed it, my heart beating fast.

'Hi,' said a familiar voice. 'This is Matthew. Uh . . . I'm sorry, but I don't think I'll be able to come to the Ball after all. Apparently there's a family trip tomorrow which I didn't know about. To Birmingham.'

'Oh,' I said, immensely relieved. 'Well, never mind.'

'I thought it might not matter so much,' said Matthew. 'Because I wasn't going to have to escort Chloe – you know?'

'Yeah, yeah, cool, of course,' I said, trying to hide my joy.

'I would like to carry on with the life coaching sessions, though,' droned Matthew. We *so* had to work on his conversational skills. 'I've bought a brown T-shirt,' he said. 'I'll wear it to Birmingham and see how it goes.'

'Yes! Good idea!' I assured him. 'And remember – if you meet anybody – don't forget to smile!'

'OK,' said Matthew gloomily. He was such a prune. However, he had now run out of things to say, and after promising to spend most of the weekend practising shaking hands with himself, he rang off.

'Matthew's dropped out,' I informed the girls. 'He has to go and show his new brown T-shirt to Birmingham.'

'Thank God for that!' sighed Chloe. Things were

gradually falling into place. We had got rid of the android. Now all we needed were Tobe and Ferg. At last Tam's mobe buzzed. She answered it with panache.

'Hi, Tobe? . . . Really? Amazing! Totally amazing! Look, don't tell Zoe I rang, for God's sake. She'd hate you to think she's all needy and stuff – but basically you've saved her life, you legend! She's downstairs now – just, uh . . . ring her and tell her you've been stood up or something, yeah? OK, babe – see you soon. Lots of love and thanks a million!'

Tam rang off and gave us the thumbs-up. I cheered. Chloe just looked mystified.

'Who were the girls, then?' she wanted to know. 'How could they just dump them like that?'

'Who cares?' I whooped. 'Don't let us down by getting all mopey about the losers, Chloe. The thing is, we ARE going to the Ball!'

Seconds later my mobe rang. I grabbed it, and turned my back on Tam and Chloe, so I wouldn't be tempted to crack up.

'Hello, my dear!' said Toby. 'Guess what? We've been dumped again! These two girls we had lined up, well basically . . . they've informed us they can't go after all. Some Bigger and Better Boys have asked them to a Bigger and Better Ball, apparently. So what was that you were talking about in your text?'

'We just had this crazy idea of going in drag. Chloe and I hire a couple of tuxedos and we go as an all-male gang. But we need you to come with us. Male solidarity, you know! How does that grab you?'

'I think it could be jolly amusing, my dear!'

That was sorted, then. I rang off, feeling relieved. But the real prob was whether the money would still be in the charity shop. We HAD to get our hands on it, first thing in the morning.

35

SATURDAY 10.00 A.M.

Fireworks, fireworks, fireworks . . .

I'd wasted hours worrying about the greedy money-grabbing women who might be running the Oxfam shop, but it turned out to be the nicest person in the world, although she did have a nose like an eagle. She beamed at us, listened to our story (the truth for once) and found the money in a jiffy. Two minutes later we were back out on the pavement with the sacred envelope containing the big bucks firmly grasped in my hot little hand.

'Thank God it was my guardian angel's shift this morning!' I said. 'Here, Tam, you look after it now.' Tam put it in her bag, but there was a slightly awkward feeling somewhere in the air, because, of course, it was partly Chloe's money, and we had come so near to losing it completely. A tingle of horror ran down my back when I imagined what it would have been like to lose it.

I had to stop brooding. Next stop was the fancy-dress-hire place. We got a bit hysterical as we walked there. I think it was the relief.

'Why stop at hiring a tux?' giggled Tam. 'You two should have a sex change. I've always wanted a brother.'

'I couldn't handle having a willy,' I said with a shudder. 'There's not enough room in my trousers as it is!'

'Horrid!' screamed Chloe. 'Gross! A root vegetable hanging off your body! Ugh!'

Suddenly my mobile laughed. I jumped. I was kind of nervy after everything that had happened in the past few hours.

'Hi, Zoe! This is Jackie!' For a moment I couldn't think who on earth Jackie was. 'Jackie Norman. I was wondering if you could possibly babysit tonight? And we still owe you for last time. The twins are longing to see you again.'

'I'm so sorry, Jackie,' I said, almost unable to conceal my glee. 'It's the Earthquake Ball tonight and we're all going.'

'Oh, no!' gasped Jackie. 'Of course! I was reading all about it in the local paper. But that means that everybody else will be going too, I suppose? What about Chloe?'

'Yes, Chloe's going,' I said. Then I had a sudden idea. 'I do know somebody who isn't, though,' I went on. 'But he's a boy.'

'Oh, a boy would be fine,' Jackie assured me. She'd have been quite happy for a boa constrictor to baby-sit her horrendous offspring, if no humans were available.

'I'll get him to ring you,' I said. Jackie sounded grateful. I stood right there on the pavement and found Scott, the strange fish-eyed nerd, in my phone's address book. I rang him. OK, it was kind of mean. But on the other hand –

'Hi,' said Scott. He didn't sound any more alive than when we'd tried to interview him.

'Scott!' I said breezily. 'This is Zoe Morris. We were talking about the life coach thing, you remember?'

'Oh yes,' said Scott, sounding panicky. 'How is – was – your dog? Did he . . . ?'

'He survived!' I assured him. 'Thanks. It was just a scratch. He's such a drama queen. But listen,

Scott . . . We haven't got the life coach thing off the ground yet, but in the meantime, I do have another job for you – only it's tonight. You wouldn't mind babysitting, I assume?'

'Oh no,' said Scott. 'I quite like – uh – kids.' Possibly because he was one himself.

I swiftly gave him the Normans' number and, after a few thanks and raptures, rang off.

I felt a bit mean for a split second, but after all, he was a terrible nerd. Besides, who knows? He might just have that X factor which the Norman twins were looking for. Maybe he'd be able to quell them with one flash of his fishy eyes.

'OK, that's all sorted,' I said. 'Poor Scott is going to take a beating tonight, babysitting for the Normans, but, babes, we are the lucky ones, cos we're going to the Ball!'

We arrived at the dress-hire place, collected some tuxedos and went off to the changing rooms. I dived into my tux, and the result was pretty amazing. I slicked back my hair, and the tuxedo and black trousers were just slightly on the large side, which was flattering.

'A sex-change op isn't compulsory,' said Tam, brushing my collar, 'but I have to admit that, if you

301

weren't my sister, and if you weren't really a girl . . .'

'Oh, shut up!' I grinned. 'Don't be so vile!' I liked the way I looked, though. It was strange. I could so easily have been born a boy. I looked a bit like a young version of Dad. How different my life would have been as a male. Chloe looked great in her tux, too.

'Would you like to see the beards and moustaches?' asked the assistant. We screamed with delight at the idea of facial hair. At least, facial hair as a fashion choice. Not, obviously, the wiry stuff that grows out of warts.

I selected a stylish goatee, and the best thing of all was that it totally covered up Nigel and his evil flashing. Chloe chose a ginger moustache to match her hair.

We left the dress-hire place loaded down with big cardboard carriers and cute little boxes for the beards and stuff. I have rarely felt more divine. We went back home to while away the time before we had to start getting ready. It was going to take a fraction of the time it usually took, because we wouldn't have to bother about shaving our legs, or getting our eyebrows just right, or trying on and discarding six hundred different necklaces.

We shared a pizza for lunch, watched a DVD, and eventually it was time to get ready to go out. I got back into my tux and waxed my hair. I was almost a babe-magnet as a boy. Weird! I'd never been a boy-magnet as a girl. I sighed. Life was harsh.

But I didn't want a sex change, because Oliver Wyatt was a boy. Boy, oh boy, was he a boy. Would he be at the Ball? Even if he was, he was sure to blank me. I still hadn't had a chance to explain about the lie I'd told about living on a farm. He obviously regarded me as a bizarre fantasist.

Toby and Fergus arrived and fell about when they saw us.

'Wow!' grinned Toby. 'You've got more testost-erone in your little finger than I have in my whole body!'

'That's not saying much.' I grinned. 'But hey! Who were those girls you dumped? Were they blondes? How did you wriggle out of that one?'

'Oh, TheyDidn'tMind,' said Fergus with a cunning grin. 'TheySaidThey'd JustAsSoonStayInTheirBoxes.'

'Their *boxes*?'

'Yeah,' explained Toby, 'they said they'd just as soon stay at home and not be inflated.'

'Inflated?' screeched Chloe. 'Not blow-up dolls?'

'Yeah.' Fergus grinned. 'WeHadThisIdea,Right? TakeACoupleOf Blow-UpDolls, Fill'EmWith Helium AndLet'EmGo!'

'Where on earth were you going to get them?' asked Chloe in disgust.

'Gary said he'd get a couple for us,' said Toby. Gary is Fergus's cousin. He's about twenty-two, and should know better.

'Well, thank God we saved you from total disgrace!' said Chloe. 'What could be more tacky and gross?'

The Ball was taking place at the Eastdene Country Club a few miles out of town. Buses had been hired to pick up everybody from our school and take us all there. Dad drove us to school.

The buses arrived, right on cue. I sat across the aisle from Jess Jordan, who was wearing a leopard-print shrug over a black dress. Her eyebrows didn't match, but she still looked completely charming, if slightly insane.

'Save the last dance for me, Jess,' I said, giving her a seductive grin and waggling my eyebrows about in a parody of masculine ogling.

'You complete and utter legend, Zoe,' said Jess. 'I *so* wish I had thought of that! I feel so lame in this boring old dress. I love your goatee!'

The Ball was magnificent. The buffet was to die for, the band was fabulous, and we all, well, had a ball. Loads of people kept coming up and saying what a great idea it was for us to go in tuxedos. And Flora Barclay told me the whole thing had raised thousands of pounds for the earthquake victims, which was good – although it did briefly make me feel intensely guilty for being at a ball at all.

I bumped into Jess again at the buffet, where we were both loading our plates with chicken wings.

'Flora says she fancies you in your tux,' whispered Jess, 'which is a tad worrying! But what I want to know is: which loos do you go to?'

'The girls', of course,' I said. 'I still haven't mastered the art of peeing standing up.'

'Yeah,' sighed Jess. 'I've often wished I could do that! Country walks would be so much easier.'

I was really enjoying being in my tux. Boys' clothes are so restful. My shoes were flat black lace-ups, of course, and no matter how much I boogied, my feet felt one hundred per cent wonderful. In a dress I'd have been constantly thinking about my appearance, and after half an hour of teetering about on heels my poor toes would have been raw hamburger.

Boys had it really lucky, in a way. Wearing a tux was liberating.

We were all having a breather and a quick drink at our table near the band, when suddenly a gruesome foursome loomed up: Beast, with Lauren Piper clinging to his arm, and Donut wrapped round a bottle blonde whose roots needed re-touching.

'Hi, guys!' said Beast cheerily. 'I'm looking for a couple of extra blokes for a rugby match next Wednesday – a flanker and a hooker.'

'If it's a flanker and a hooker you want,' I said, 'I suggest you look in the mirror.' I don't quite understand rugby talk, but it sounded something like a put-down.

Beast laughed, winked at me, and moved off. Lauren looked triumphant.

'She'll soon find out what he's like,' said Chloe, and sighed. And then – she blushed! Again! I was going to have to watch her, and no mistake. What's more, the blush clashed with her ginger moustache. Pink and orange are a bit too lively together, in my opinion.

However, Chloe's tuxedo seemed to be offering some protection: I didn't think even Beast would have the nerve to hit on her while she was in boy's clothing, especially as he had another girl actually attached to his arm.

'I'm going to the loos to check on my moustache,' said Chloe. It seemed as if she wanted a moment by herself. I decided to go out on to the terrace to get a bit of fresh air.

As I arrived outside, an explosion of fireworks lit up the country park: the lake, the woods, the sky. Everything seemed very beautiful. The whole evening was just divine. I was so glad we'd made it.

'Hi there,' said a voice in the dark. I turned round. It was Oliver.

My heart performed a double somersault, my face boiled, and my braces burst, but luckily some fireworks went off at the same time, and the darkness covered my blushes.

'Nice tux,' he added. The ghost of a smile crossed his handsome face.

'Listen,' I said. The time had come. 'I'm sorry. It was all a lie about living on a farm. For reasons which must remain private.'

Oliver was quiet. We watched a few more rockets soar above the woods. My heart was racing.

'Well, curiously,' he replied, 'I was also lying about wanting to be a vet. For reasons which must also remain a mystery.'

There was a long, long, pause. Before, just my heart had been racing, with panic and excitement. Now my brain was whirling as well. What was he trying to say? Something? Anything? Nothing?

The firework display came to an end, and there was a gunpowdery smell on the night air.

'I'd ask you to dance,' said Oliver, 'but people would talk.'

I grinned, although I wasn't completely sure what I was grinning at. Just then, with disastrous timing, Toby and Fergus lurched out of the ballroom behind us.

'Hello, chaps!' Toby grinned. 'How's the goatee holding up, Zoe – or should I call you Joey?'

I muttered some rubbish about how I was going to wear it for the rest of my life. For once, I wished Toby and Fergus would get lost. If they'd known I had a crush on Oliver, they might have tiptoed off tactfully instead of ruining my almost-magic moment.

Oliver didn't stay long after Toby and Fergus appeared. He just said, 'See you,' gave me a secret kind of nod – or was it, perhaps, just an ordinary nod? – and strolled off into the darkness.

Toby and Fergus were arguing about whether all vodka comes from Russia, or something equally ludicrous, but I found it impossible to concentrate on anything anyone said. That amazing revelation from Oliver just kept whizzing round and round in my head. It seemed to give off dazzling sparks. He'd been lying about wanting to be a vet? What on earth had he meant by it? I hardly dared think.

The fireworks had been a sign that the evening was over. But it also felt like a prelude, as if something was beginning. Or was I imagining things? On the bus on the way home, I slipped into a kind of dream. Had Oliver been trying to tell me something? If so, what?

Maybe he was gay – and he only fancied me if I was dressed as a boy! A terrible thought. But I was quite willing to become a transvestite if that was what was required. A transsexual, even.

Mum and Dad had gone to bed when I got home, but Tam was still up, and we had a cup of hot choc together. I told her what a fantastic time we'd had, and about Oliver's mysterious words.

'It must mean he was only *pretending* to be interested in being a vet,' said Tam, 'because he fancied you so much, and when he heard you lived on a farm he saw it as a chance to get to know you.'

'God, no, Tam!' I said, my heart looping the loop, 'No, no, that can't be true! Do you really think so?'

'Of course!' said Tam, grinning. 'What else could he possibly mean?'

After we'd talked about how mysterious Oliver was for about half an hour, I began to feel really shattered.

'Bedtime,' said Tam. 'But oh – this is for you, Zoe.' She reached inside her handbag and got out the envelope with the money in. She put it on the table and pushed it towards me.

'What?' I stammered. 'How come?'

'I had a little talk with Dad after Mum had gone to bed,' whispered Tam. 'It's all sorted. Dad's given me a loan instead. Not a word to Mum, though!'

'Really?' I stared at the envelope, relief beginning to wash over me. All those awkward feelings I'd been having were swept away. I could give Toby and Chloe and Fergus their money back, and things could get back to normal, with no edgy, guilty anxiety about how and when they were going to get repaid.

'I felt so awful, borrowing from your friends,' said Tam. Her eyes filled with tears. 'Awful, awful! Like I was some sad sicko – it was like, getting into trouble through my own stupidity, and then stealing from kids' piggy banks, for God's sake.'

'We're not kids!' I snapped, in a kind of minor huff.

'Well, obviously not!' said Tam. 'Like, you guys are actually managing to save up for something, unlike my idiot self. I just let things get totally out of control. God, I'm so ashamed! But now it's just a deal between me and Dad.'

'Good,' I said. 'It's better that way.'

'I'm still doing poverty chic, and getting a job at Easter, and all that,' said Tam, 'only I secretly pay Dad back instead of you guys. But I will take you all out for a meal, just to say thank you for your support. It meant so much to me.' A tear ran down her cheek.

'I'm glad,' I said. 'It's better like this.' I gave her a hug.

'Uhhh . . . it's weird hugging you with your beard and stuff on,' she said, breaking away with a slight frisson and a tearful grin. 'Just promise me you won't tell Mum about the mess I got myself into.'

'Why would I?' I said. Deep inside, complete relaxation was taking over me. I was now ready to sleep for ten hours, and dream about Oliver non-stop.

'How was your evening, anyway, Tam?' I asked, as we cleared away the mugs.

'Oh, nice. Mum and Dad took me out for an Italian meal,' said Tam. 'Mum was rabbiting on about this all-male production of *Hamlet* you're going to. She seemed really excited about it. What was it again – an all-male production, in Russian?'

A small but perfectly formed panic sprang up again in my rather overworked ribcage. There was still a lot of work to be done before my life was totally sorted. I had to sort out the lie to Mum about the all-male *Hamlet* trip. Plus I had, at some stage, to phone Scott and find out if he had survived the Norman twins. But tomorrow was another day.

'Tam,' I said, 'I'm not going to the all-male *Hamlet*. Mum just thinks I am. I used it as an excuse to get enough money to come up and see you at uni. So it's your job to think of a way of getting me off the hook. By tomorrow morning.'

'OK,' said Tam, yawning. 'Your word is my command. You're the best sister I've got. Sorry, I mean the best sister in the world – it's official.'

'See you in the morning,' I said.

'Sweet dreams!' she whispered.

We parted on the landing: she to her solemn, old,

disapproving teddy bear, and me to my smiley, gay, fluffy one. I knew Bruce was dying to hear all about the Ball, but to be honest, I was in such a fabulous state of turmoil, I didn't know where to begin.

Read on for a taster of
Girls, Muddy, Moody Yet Magnificent
by Sue Limb

Zoe and Chloe. Chloe and Zoe. Best friends together unless there are boys around, of course in which case it's every girl for herself!

What? Four hundred and fifty? Just for a caravan for a week?' Chloe's voice soared upwards in a hysterical shriek. It was the first day of the summer hols, and we were surfing the Newquay websites. We had been dreaming of this holiday for ages, but where were we going to stay? Foolishly, although we'd been fantasising about it for so long, we hadn't got around to arranging any of the practical details.

'We could share with Toby and Fergus . . .' I suggested. 'Between four, it'd only be, uh . . . a hundred and something.'

'*Only?*' wailed Chloe. 'Anyway, we can't share a caravan with Tobe and Ferg. They would, like, see us in our pants and, even worse, we would see them in *their* pants.'

'What sort of pants do you think Ferg wears?' I giggled. Toby and Fergus are our best boy mates at school and, with any luck, we would never get to see their pants for the rest of our entire lives. Tobe's very camp, and Ferg's very tiny, so they're a bit of a comedy duo, but they'd already been a lot more organised than us, getting holiday jobs and saving up loads.

'Ferg's pants . . . ?' Chloe mused. 'Hmmm . . . possibly a pattern of cute yellow mice wearing top hats?'

'Yeah.' I grinned. 'As for Toby, it's got to be pink with lace edges.'

'God, he's so outrageous!' laughed Chloe. 'Isn't it weird how some guys can be camp without being gay?'

'And vice versa,' I mused. 'But, hey! Focus, Chloe! Back to the pressing issue of our accommodation!'

'Chill out! You're such a Victorian governess!' wailed Chloe in mock torment.

'Maybe that explains it all!' I had a moment of revelation. 'Maybe in a previous existence I literally *was* your Victorian governess!'

'Maybe we should get hypnotised and do past-lives regression,' said Chloe eagerly. 'I'm sure I can remember your starchy collar and luxuriant moustache!'

I fingered my upper lip anxiously. The awful thing is, I sometimes think I *really am* getting a moustache. I once spent ten minutes in the bathroom with my dad's shaving mirror and a torch and I detected more than a peachy bloom on my upper lip: it was a *wheat field*. By the time I'm forty I'll need a combine harvester to de-fuzz myself.

'I *know* you were my governess!' giggled Chloe. 'I remember the twang of your corsets! You were still a virgin at sixty-five!'

'Well, you were a crazy Victorian nymphomaniac,' I quipped.

'That is totally unfair!' yelled Chloe hysterically. 'OK, I was a nymphomaniac, but I was so *not* crazy!'

'You had hair two metres long and mad red flashing eyes,' I told her. 'I had to manacle you to the bedpost whenever the footman was passing.'

Chloe giggled and opened a new web page from the Newquay Accommodation website.

'Oh my God!' wailed Chloe. 'Look! It says, *"Our caravans are available to families and over-eighteens only"*!' A huge wave of fatigue swept over me – and I *so* hate huge waves of all sorts.

'Forget it, then,' I said, fingering my chin. There's a spot there called Nigel and he emerges every month along with premenstrual tension. I was feeling tense now. 'Hey, babe – maybe we should leave it till tomorrow.' I had a horrid feeling that the search for accommodation was going to end badly. We'd been feverishly longing for this trip for ages. Everybody at school was going, or said they were: it was practically compulsory to go to Newquay this year.

What if it all went pear-shaped? I slipped into one of my nightmare scenarios. I have them about six times a day.

If we ever got to Newquay, we'd have to sleep on a park bench. No, that would be way too comfy: we'd end up sleeping on the pavement. Dogs would pee on us in the night. Drunks would fall on us. We would be mugged by gangs of feral street-children.

But aside from all this hysterical fantasy stuff, there was a real problem, a huge issue that we'd been kind of ignoring. I think it's called the Elephant in the Room: a really massive thing that nobody dares mention. I knew I was going to have to be the one to broach the subject.

'Hey, wait a min!' said Chloe, still ripping through endless Newquay web pages. 'What about hostels?' She typed *Newquay hostels* into Google. 'Wow!' she breathed. 'This looks great! It says it's the fave place for surfers! And they don't have a curfew! We could pull a couple of heavenly boys and sit out on the beach with them, all night.'

'If we're going to sit out on the beach with heavenly boys all night,' I grinned, 'why bother with a hostel at all?' Somehow, in my imagination, one of the heavenly boys was faintly familiar: tall and dark and mysterious-looking. I picked up a pen and idly wrote the name Oliver on my arm like a kind of tattoo.

'We could live on the beach!' yelled Chloe in excitement. 'We could build ourselves a house of sand! We could become mermaids!' Then, suddenly, everything changed. 'Oh, no!' Her fingers came to a halt, and all the excitement died in her voice. 'How totally unfair!'

'What?' I asked, full of dread. I was already convinced that nobody in the whole of Newquay would accept two under-eighteens on their own. We'd have to disguise ourselves as our own grandmothers.

'*They* don't accept anybody under eighteen, either,' growled Chloe. 'Tight or what? An Eighteen-and-Over hostel!'

'What kind of lifestyle do they have in these hostels?' I shook my head in disbelief. 'A life of rampant sex and violence?'

'Pornographic breakfasts?' suggested Chloe, getting into it. 'Two fried eggs and a sausage?'

'Served by gothic wenches in bondage gear?' I added. 'A severed head on the mantelpiece – of a guest who hasn't paid his bill?'

'En suite torture chambers!' giggled Chloe. 'Oh look!' She was still racing through the web pages at the speed of light. 'This one says, "*Guests aged between sixteen and eighteen will be accepted only if accompanied by a letter of consent from their parents*"!'

Chloe turned to me, alarm flickering in her green eyes. This was the Elephant in the Room: we hadn't told our parents.

'We're going to have to tell them some time,' I said. 'Why not now?'

Right on cue, we heard Chloe's mum's key in the lock.

Girls, Muddy, Moody Yet Magnificent
OUT IN JANUARY 2010